Patricia Fisher: Ship's Detective

Patricia Fisher: Ship's Detective

Book 1

Steve Higgs

Publisher: Steve Higgs

Dedication

While writing this story, I attended a conference for independent authors in Las Vegas. It was the first time I had been away from my family in more than two years, and I was on the very first flight into the fabled city of sin from the UK for six hundred days.

With nothing better to do, my default is always to write, but five hours into the flight, the battery on my laptop was exhausted, so I switched to using a notepad and pen. I could type my words up later and that was better than stopping now that I was in a flow with the story.

My pen ran out of ink three hours after that, and I still had more than two hours of flight time. The lady sitting next to me heard my chuckling as the pen I brought along ran dry, and kindly gave me one of hers.

This book is dedicated to her, the random lady in seat 45F.

Josephine Somers

Table of Contents

The Trigger

Antonio Bardem never imagined this day would actually come. The monthly retainer fee he received was a nice bonus and it helped to pay his bills. His boss didn't know about it and never would; not that Antonio believed he was doing anything wrong – it wasn't like it was a bribe.

It kind of was though, and he knew it.

Did this mean the payments would stop? He figured they probably would and that was disappointing, but what could he do? He allowed himself to idly consider not passing the message on. If he pretended the trigger hadn't just happened, he could continue getting the money. Otherwise, he would have to explain to his wife why his monthly income had reduced.

But he remembered the phone call he received when he took the job. The old guy he replaced told him to expect it – what was his name? Antonio dredged his brain to find the name of the man working as the professor's research assistant before he took the job, but it wouldn't come. It didn't matter, of course.

Whatever his name was, he had pulled Antonio to one side on his first day, checking all around to be sure they were not being overheard before telling him that he would be contacted by a man who would ask him to watch out for something specific.

It happened the following day, but it wasn't a phone call, the man was waiting outside Antonio's house, there to deliver an offer that sounded more like a threat. There was no question that Antonio would do what the man wanted, the subtext in his words had been that the next man would if Antonio refused. Antonio didn't want to think about why the job would suddenly be vacant for a new man.

Besides, it was a harmless thing he was being asked to do. Watch out for something ... anything pertaining to some old ship called the San Jose and call the number he was given if anything ever showed up.

It happened less than an hour ago, sending a spike of trepidation through Antonio's gut when he realised he needed to make the call.

So, reluctantly, and with his heart thumping in his chest, he dialled the number the man gave him more than three years ago.

'This is Silvestre,' the man had a strange way of speaking and his clipped words were enunciated in a manner that suggested he was born into wealth and was used to commanding people.

'Good evening, Senor Silvestre. This is Antonio at the National Museum of Brazil. I work under ...'

'I know who you are,' Silvestre cut right over what Antonio was trying to say, spiking the nervousness Antonio already felt.

Antonio had wanted to leave the building to make the phone call, but knew his absence would draw questions.

'An artefact has been found?' Silvestre pressed for confirmation, his voice ripe with anticipation.

'The professor himself confirmed it earlier,' he whispered into the phone, peering out from the nook he was in when he thought he heard someone coming. With his heart hammering in his chest, he said, 'Professor Noriega got very excited when he saw what it was, Senor. He called it the cross of Eduardo Vega.'

At the other end of the line, Xavier Silvestre closed his eyes and stilled his breathing. It had finally happened, but now he needed to act fast.

There were things that had to happen in quick succession, and it started with finding out who had brought the artefact into the museum.

'I do not know the man's name, Senor,' Antonio replied apologetically.

Silvestre offered a year's wages for him to stop whatever he was doing and find out. He wanted a name and the address for where the man was staying. A phone number if possible.

Unable to believe the man's generosity or his luck, all Antonio's concerns for the loss of income evaporated in an instant. He promised to call back the moment he had obtained the name of the man who arrived with the cross an hour ago. He was still here, talking with the professor about where he had discovered the jewel encrusted gold cross.

Antonio did not know why the cross was significant; he was just a lowly assistant, barely trusted to fetch coffee for the professor, but with a fat bonus looming, details of the cross and why Senor Silvestre was so interested in it were unimportant details. He would tail the man to his hotel and get his name and phone number from them.

On the other side of the Atlantic, in his sprawling ranch in Spain, Xavier Silvestre summoned his own assistant, a lumbering, monosyllabic ox of a man called Gomez. He needed his plane to be made ready and his bags to be packed – he might not be home again for some time.

As Gomez departed, Silvestre turned his eyes toward the giant oil painting dominating one wall of his office. The eighteenth-century galleon had been an obsession for more years than he could remember.

The San Jose supposedly went to the bottom when it left Peru, laden with treasure and bound for Spain. Its escort of navy frigates were delayed but the captain chose to sail anyway, expecting the lighter, faster ships to catch him.

It happened during the time of the Spanish Succession when the British cornered and sank the San Jose off the coast of Colombia. Or so British records claim. No survivors were ever found, nor was the ship itself, but the captain of another Spanish vessel claimed he saw the San Jose anchored off the coast of Morocco.

Legends grew of pirates attacking the San Jose while the captain and crew were attempting to steal the cargo. What had become of it no one knew, but the ship was never found, and the treasure was yet to be recovered.

Silvestre had been captivated by the tale when he first heard it and had poured millions into researching any slim lead that might reveal where the pirates had taken it. The millions spent hardly mattered, estimates of the treasure's current value ran into the billions.

It was out there. He knew it was. Having explored every lead until it ran dry, he left triggers at different institutes around the globe. If a piece of the treasure ever came to light, he would hear about it.

Thirty years of his life had been spent pursuing the world's greatest treasure. Now aged fifty-seven, he finally had the lead he needed. The man in Rio de Janeiro was going to tell him where he found the cross whether he wanted to or not.

Passport Thieves – 4650 Miles from Brazil Onboard the Aurelia

The scream of outrage drew the attention of everyone in the restaurant. Three yards to my front, a lady in her forties with frizzy blonde hair and dressed for a day ashore, was spinning around to see who was there.

I have been tracking a team of passport thieves for almost a week now. They were slick, and it had taken me a long time to identify the first of them. I could have pounced at that point, and my judgement was questioned when I opted to not do so. However, I wanted all of them and believed I could catch them in one fell swoop if we timed it right.

I had my eyes locked on a Turkish man in his early thirties. He went by the name of Halit Saat. I suspected the name to be fake, especially since the man was in the business of stealing passports.

He was operating with a team of three, two of whom I had been able to identify thus far. The first of them had just jostled the lady with the frizzy blonde hair as if accidentally bumping into her on his way across the restaurant. I had watched them perform this routine four times now in different parts of the ship.

The accidental bump caused the lady and her husband to momentarily stop their forward motion. The jostling was timed so that Halit would arrive and be able to plunge a hand in and out of her pocketbook so swiftly that all she would notice was someone passing close to her.

I had just witnessed that happening and the passport was now in Halit's hands. He continued walking, never breaking stride, and in the space of a second had switched the passport from one hand to the other and was surreptitiously holding it out for the third member of the team to take.

Usually, when they struck, the victim failed to notice anything had happened until they came to look for their passport some time later. However, this was one of the occasions when the victim reacted instantly. Partly this was because my team and I have been blanket messaging all passengers to be on the alert and what to look out for. Before my eyes she was spinning around, reacting to the close proximity of the two men and reaching for her pocketbook to check that nothing had been taken.

This was where the slickness of their operation came into play. Were she to grab Halit and accuse him of taking her passport, she would find him empty handed and claiming his innocence as the third man made off on a separate trajectory.

However, on this occasion, the third man did not attempt to go anywhere. Instead, he grabbed Halit's right arm and slapped a handcuff on it.

I was standing close enough that I got to see the white of Halit's eyes as the shock of capture hit them. He was looking at his wrist in disbelief, then up at his fellow criminal to question what on earth he was playing at. A smile tugged at the corners of my mouth when I saw his eyes flare even wider.

The man wearing his colleague's clothes – all it took to fool Halit - was my own Lieutenant Pippin.

Anders Pippin, the youngest member of a team of security officers assigned to assist me, had the passport, which gave us the evidence, and we had two of the team in custody, having taken out the man Halit expected to hand off to just a few minutes ago.

That left just one to catch.

I locked eyes with the Jostler. He was backing away from the lady with the frizzy blonde hair and his face was filled with panic.

'You are caught,' I stated, my words hard as I stepped forward. The crowd was parting, but before I could say 'There's no point in running', guess what he chose to do?

An exasperated sigh escaped my lips as I watched him twist to face away from me and take off like Carl Lewis.

I screamed for him to stop, a fruitless action that he paid not the slightest heed too. Accepting my fate, I kicked off my heels and gave pursuit.

What's that? Who am I? Yes, I probably ought to bring you up to speed, I suppose.

My name is Patricia Fisher. A bunch of months ago I caught my husband of thirty years doing something with my best friend of which I highly disapproved. Unable to think straight at the time, I ran away from the situation rather than deal with it.

I ran all the way to Southampton where I spent almost every penny in my husband's bank account to buy a cruise ticket that would take me all the way around the world.

I got a little bit squiffy that first night drowning my sorrows in gin, and awoke to find myself accused of murder and embroiled in a decades old priceless jewel theft. All alone, and feeling like I hadn't a friend in the world, I was rescued from the pit of my despair by a butler who came with the suite I was staying in and his BFF gym instructor friend.

The three of us solved our way out of trouble, narrowly avoiding getting shot several times along the way. One thing led to another and long story short, I discovered that I have a knack for solving mysteries. The priceless jewel turned out to belong to the third richest man on the planet, the Maharaja of Zangrabar, who proved to be rather grateful when I returned it.

He became my benefactor, and if I chose to, I could live a life of absolute luxury and fill my days with shopping and parties and artistic pursuits. However, I think I would find that rather boring, and I've made a lot of good friends in the months since I ran away from home who are almost exclusively involved in solving crimes – precisely where my skills lie. It's rather exciting most of the time.

My boyfriend is the captain of the ship, a ridiculously handsome man who has generously chosen to lavish me with his romantic inclinations. My life is nothing short of wonderful.

Except for right now, of course, because now I had to run, and at fifty-three I'm not a massive fan of chasing men in their twenties.

I have a team of five working with me, three lieutenants and a Lieutenant Commander, plus my personal assistant, Sam, who wears the rank of ensign. They are all exceptional individuals, and they support me in my role as the ship's detective.

Lieutenant Schneider, a six-foot goodness knows what Austrian who looks like he's been hewn out of oak, had been positioned by the door to the restaurant to ensure that he could head off any of the passport thief team if they chose to run. Lieutenant Bhukari, the one female in my team, was in the crowd, but on the wrong side to intercept the runner. I saw her begin to move, a blur in plain clothes as she shot across the room.

That left Lieutenant Commander Martin Baker, Lieutenant Deepa Bhukari's husband, but as he stepped out to intercept the Jostler, he made his move too obvious. The Jostler dropped his shoulders to slam into Baker's midriff and we all heard an 'Oooof 'of outrushing air as Baker was bowled over backwards.

'Stop!' I yelled. 'Where is it you think you're going to go? You're on a ship!'

His behaviour was not unusual, this was perhaps the third time this week we had been forced to chase someone as they attempted to evade us. All around the ship were mile upon mile of open ocean and yet they seemed to think they could somehow escape us.

My hope that Lieutenant Schneider would catch him at the door was thwarted by the man choosing a different route. We were sailing into Gibraltar, and would be docking within the next hour, hence the lady with the frizzy blonde hair being dressed for a day of tourism ashore.

The man we were chasing was heading straight for a door on the portside, some of which were open to create a pleasant breeze through the restaurant.

None of us were going to get to him before he got outside, I could see that already. Would he leap over the railing? We were on the top deck, which made it more than one hundred feet to the water below. I had seen one individual jump and survive and in truth if the Jostler chose to jump, fishing him out of the water would be a simple enough task.

Of course, running as fast as my little legs could carry me and attempting to work out where he was going to go, my attention was not on what was around me. Consequently, I collided with one of the stewards as he turned away from a table with a large tray of dirty breakfast plates.

A sound approximate to that of a one-man-band being launched into space echoed all around me as the silver tray with the crockery, cutlery and leftover food it held, shot into the air.

I rebounded to land hard on my bottom and stared into the space above my head as the tray and all that was on it reached the apex of its ascent, obeyed the laws of gravity, and came hurtling back toward me and the unlucky steward. I was wearing my new top, the one from the boutique on the eighteenth deck. It was a pricey item I had ummed and arred about buying for almost a week until convincing myself I deserved it. Now watching food rain down from the air above me, and unable to get out of the way, I suspected this was the only time I would ever get to wear it.

When the breakfast crescendo ended with a final, almost comical, ping of a fork landing on the silver tray, my assistant, Sam, skidded to a halt at my side.

'Wow, Mrs Fisher!' he gasped. 'You look like a Picasso painting!' he chuckled.

Sam didn't mean to be insensitive, he has Downs Syndrome and doesn't always articulate his thoughts in the best manner. I hired him because he is wonderful to be around and because his uniqueness allows him to see things in a completely different way to everyone else.

On several occasions that has proven to be pivotal in an investigation.

A quick glance down at my top confirmed it was going in the bin. My left boob had found a big blob of ketchup somehow and there was a piece of bacon sticking out of my cleavage. I had a smear of egg yolk on my right shoulder and could feel something sticky on my face.

I chose not to think too hard about what that might be.

With a grunt of apology to the steward, I accepted Sam's hand to get up and we started running again. There were astonished passengers staring at me, many of them rising to their feet to better observe the spectacle.

Ahead of me, the Jostler shot through the door and angled hard left, running towards the aft of the ship since we were all the way up at the bow. If we lost sight of him, he could easily lose us in the maze that was the world's largest luxury cruise liner. If he then chose to hide, it could take days and endless manhours to find him. Worse yet, when we docked, it was not beyond belief that he might find a way to escape the ship without us detecting him.

We needed to catch him now. With a gasp of air to refill my lungs - I was out of breath and struggling to speak - I managed to shout to Lieutenant Bhukari, 'Keep going!' She had paused to make sure I was okay, but shot after our runner again.

I followed her out of the door with Sam at my shoulder.

There was fifty yards between me and the man I wanted to catch. Lieutenant Bhukari was ten yards ahead of me and leaving me in her wake. Like everyone else I worked with, she was more than two decades my junior and significantly fitter.

We raced along the deck, swerving around passengers who squealed and gasped in astonishment as we ran between them. They were used to seeing the occasional jogger keeping fit on deck - witnessing an all-out chase was unusual to say the least.

I came around the edge of the superstructure that contained the upper deck accommodation, restaurants, and other facilities, and into the upper deck sun terrace. There were people catching the sun already - kids played in the pool and contented couples read magazines or books or chatted happily on sun loungers.

Going too fast to change direction, I leapt over a woman on her sun lounger, hearing a shriek of surprise from her as I landed on the other side to continue my pursuit.

The Jostler was showing us a fast pair of heels and we were not going to catch him unless something occurred to slow him down.

I heard a whistle, the sound coming from Lieutenant Bhukari, as she signalled to someone ahead of us. I couldn't see who it was and ducked my head left and right as I attempted to catch a glimpse of who she had spotted.

Except, once again that meant I was not looking where I was going until a woman's scream pierced my ears. Casting my eyes about to see what drama I had failed to notice, I also screamed when I spotted the tiny toddler directly in my path.

The boy, no more than eighteen months old, held an ice cream lazily in one hand where the melting vanilla goodness dripped and slid over his fingers. He looked up with a terrified expression as the madwoman running hell for leather came straight at him.

I screamed in horror and threw myself into the air. The panicked manoeuvre carried me harmlessly over the child's head, but I had no control over my body when I came back to the deck. I landed awkwardly, my inertia carrying me onwards to careen into an empty sunbed. I jumped again to try to avoid falling on it, but misjudged where I needed to put my feet so came back down on the head end.

It flipped instantly.

The foot end hit me on the back of the head as I stumbled forward and the combined effect was sufficient to throw me forward, my arms pinwheeling as I pitched over.

Can you guess what was in front of me?

That's right, the swimming pool.

I plunged in headfirst, out of breath and gasping for air even before my scream of horror was cut off by the blissfully cool water. I went under, but bobbed up just in time to see a woman in her eighties step out in front of the Jostler's path. Her handbag was scribing an arc upwards from her ankles to connect beneath his chin.

The effect was as if he had run headfirst into a steel girder. His head stopped instantly while momentum carried the rest of his body forward. His legs lifted from the deck to return, along with the rest of his body, a second or so later when gravity reclaimed him.

I was trying to tread water, and paddle to the side, but seeing my distress, two lifeguards had dived in to save me. The crew members on pool duty today had hold of my arms in their attempt to save my life. Little did they know the most dangerous thing in my life was me and my clumsiness.

'Keep, calm, Madam!' one of the lifeguards begged. I was fighting them both, attempting to get my limbs free because I wanted to get out of the water.

I knew who the old lady was, and someone needed to get to the Jostler before she did any more damage.

Fighting the lifeguards as I was, I lost my footing and ducked under again just as I was taking a breath. Now coughing and spluttering, I had no choice but to let the lifeguards help me to the side.

I was a drowned rat - hair and makeup stuck to my face and my clothes dripping to form a puddle around my feet as I slogged across the sun terrace like a swamp monster. Bewildered passengers gawped at me, and those in my path happily stepped aside rather than risk entering the circle of doom that seems to surround me.

At least I didn't have to rush. The action was over, and the criminal had been caught. By the time I arrived at the Jostler's location, Lieutenants Bhukari and Schneider had the man sitting up and in cuffs. Lieutenant Commander Baker was radioing for assistance, and the old lady who had stopped the runner dead in his tracks was sitting on a sun lounger from where she was fruitlessly lecturing the Turkish man in English.

'You ought to be ashamed of yourself, young man. Stealing passports. Whatever were you going to do with them? I shall pray for you at church this week,' she advised. As if noticing me for the first time, the old lady looked up at my face. 'Ooh, what happened to you, Patricia?' she asked.

'Mrs Fisher fell in the pool, Gran!' Sam laughed.

Because of what I told you about Sam earlier, he needs a live-in assistant. His grandmother, Gloria, was only too happy to volunteer for the role. I understood why - she was enjoying an all-expenses trip around the planet aboard a luxury cruise ship. Sam has his own accommodation in which his grandmother also resides, and she takes care of his daily needs while he works alongside me on the ship.

He was accorded the honorary rank of ensign and gets to wear a uniform. I believe his employment to be a public relations manoeuvre on the part of Purple Star, the cruise line who own the Aurelia. However, since everyone seems to get what they want from the deal, I see no reason to challenge it.

The Jostler looked dazed, I noted, remembering how effectively his forward motion had been stopped by Gloria's handbag. Narrowing my eyes, I looked at Sam's granny.

'Gloria, what have you got in your handbag?'

She offered me an innocent face.

'The usual things: hairbrush, suntan lotion, my purse,' she mumbled something after that which none of us were able to hear.

'I'm sorry,' I smiled sweetly at her. 'Could you repeat that last part? I didn't quite catch it.'

She huffed and let her shoulders droop in defeat.

'A house brick,' she repeated, but this time at a volume we could all hear. To accentuate her words, she opened her handbag to show us.

Baker asked the question first. 'Mrs Chalk where did you find a house brick on board a cruise ship?'

She looked at him like he was being stupid. 'I brought it with me, of course. I'm an old lady. I need a little extra something on hand in case I have to protect myself.'

I had to stifle the laugh that erupted from my core and then suffered a bout of choking that drew a frown from Sam's grandmother. I rejoined the Aurelia and took up my new post as Ship's Detective two weeks ago. Sam and his gran arrived at the same time, but where she was supposed to be looking after him, it quickly became clear that Gloria was reliving her youth instead.

Cruise ships attract a lot of older persons and she fitted right into that demographic. There were parties to go to, bingo and other pensioner appropriate activities to join in with, and though I was yet to prove it, I suspected she had become something of a sexual predator.

There were many older men on board, travelling with their families but otherwise effectively single. If a person felt so inclined, there were fresh lovers arriving every time the ship docked.

Lieutenant Commander Baker touched my shoulder.

'Mrs Fisher, I've got Lieutenant Beverly from engineering on the line.' He offered me his radio.

I almost questioned why the call hadn't come through on my radio, then remembered I had elected to take it swimming.

I thumbed the button to speak. 'Patricia here. Do you need something? I've just made an arrest.'

There was a brief pause before Lieutenant Beverly's voice crackled over the airwaves.

'You are going to want to come down to deck three, Mrs Fisher. I have something for you to see.' I was about to question his cryptic response and request he make himself clearer when he added, 'It's a secretary situation.'

My next breath caught in my throat as all around me, my team looked my way. We all knew the codeword meant Lieutenant Beverly had discovered a dead passenger. I wanted to get out of my wet things, but that was going to have to wait.

As I hurried away, taking Sam with me, but leaving Baker and the others to deal with the passport thieves, the question at the top of the list was all to do with what a passenger might have been doing that far down in the ship's hull.

Stowaway?

'How long would you say he has been dead?' I asked the question and glanced at the man leaning over the body. Dr Hideki Nakamura was a medical student and driving a cab in Tokyo to pay his tuition when I met him several months ago. He hit it off with my gym instructor friend, Barbie, and the two were a firm couple now.

A confluence of events created a position for him to practice medicine onboard the ship when he graduated, and he leapt at the chance.

The young doctor was on his knees, crouching over the body to examine it. There could be no question that we were looking at a murder. There was a knife sticking out of his chest right above his heart.

I think it says a lot about my life, or at least the recent portion of it, that I was able to stare down at the dead body without freaking out. In many ways I am unrecognisable from the woman I was less than a year ago.

In the last six months I have seen altogether too many dead bodies, most of them murder victims. Each of them had a story to tell and this one would be no different. Unlike before when I had investigated occurrences aboard the ship partly out of curiosity, and partly because I needed to solve each case so that I could stay one step ahead of the criminal, it was now entirely my job to determine what had happened to the man.

I had already established that the victim was carrying nothing we could use to identify him, and it was obvious from the condition of the body, that he had been dead for some time. Hence the question I had just posed to Hideki.

Dr Hideki Nakamura sat back on his haunches, sucking a little air through his teeth as he pondered my question.

'I shall need to conduct some tests, Patricia, but if you want a guess, I would say it's at least two weeks.'

I shook my head from side to side but kept my eyes on the body. The man was dressed in raggedy clothes with mismatched socks and one shoe missing. I judged his age to be somewhere around thirty and his height to be a shade under six feet. He was Caucasian, and skinny to the point that he looked to have been starving.

However, the standout feature anyone would notice first was that he was an albino. His sightless eyes were eerily red, and his hair – eyebrows, beard ... everything - were so white they were almost translucent. His skin had been burned by the sun at some point in the days before his death, the evidence of scabbing on his ears and neck left as evidence. It didn't tell me much of anything that I could use.

To find out more, an autopsy would be required, the gruesome task falling almost certainly to Hideki, the most junior of the doctors on board the Aurelia.

The albino had been killed long enough ago that I considered the likelihood of his killer still being on board to be almost nil. Would I even be able to determine what had happened to him?

I knew I would spend a good portion of today going through the passenger manifest in an attempt to find out who the mystery man might be. No one had reported a loved one missing, and we did not get many people travelling alone. The cleaning staff onboard were astute enough to have reported if it was clear a cabin had not been slept in for several nights, so I was left questioning whether the man might in fact be a stowaway.

That he had been found several decks below the lowest passenger deck, and in a rarely visited area of the ship's hull suggested that might very well be the case. This would make him even harder to identify. Nevertheless, it was my job.

Lieutenant Beverly had remained with the body after a member of the engineering team working under him had reported the find. He was there still, loitering a few yards away, duty demanding he could not abandon the unpleasant task of dealing with the body.

With a twitch of his muscles, Hideki bounced up and onto his feet.

'I'll have stewards take him to the crew medical area. I don't think we should put him anywhere near where the passengers might see.' As if talking to himself, Hideki remarked, 'I wonder when anyone last performed an autopsy on this ship?'

I didn't know the answer to his question, and didn't feel it required a comment. Leaving Lieutenant Beverly to guard the body until the stewards arrived with a stretcher to take it away, I began making my way back towards the elevator.

I was getting cold, my clothes still soaked, though they had mostly stopped dripping now. I got looks from passengers when I made my way through the ship to find an elevator on my way down to meet Hideki and the body. I had been wringing wet and covered in bits of breakfast detritus. However, no one among the crew thought it necessary to comment when they saw me. This is probably because getting covered in gunk, or somehow ending up naked is not particularly unusual for me.

Sam asked, 'What's next, Mrs Fisher?' He posed the question while we waited for the elevator to arrive on deck three.

I did not need to think before answering, 'Next is a hot shower and a change of clothes, Sam. I rather think I'd like to get dry before I do anything else today. We shall have to wait for Dr Nakamura to complete his autopsy before we will know anything about the poor man we just found, but I imagine much of the rest of this morning will be taken up by paperwork as we deal with the team of passport thieves we've just caught.'

'Are we going ashore?' Sam wanted to know, revealing what he had really been asking me.

Until I hired him, Sam had never really been anywhere. He lived in a small village in Kent with his parents and had very few hopes for his future. Now he was in paid employment and getting to see and do things that he had probably never even dreamed might be possible. Of course he wanted to get ashore and see what there was to see.

The elevator pinged and the doors swished open, revealing the empty silver box inside. I stepped over the threshold, and pressed the button for deck twenty, the top deck where my suite could be found.

'You should collect your granny and get ashore as soon as you can, Sam. Don't forget to change out of your uniform though,' I reminded him. Sam had a number of skills that I might call upon, but filling in paperwork was not one of them. We would need to hand our suspects off to the local authority at the port and provide the case we had made against them. Thereafter, our involvement in their detainment and what would happen to them next ended.

Acting upon my instructions, with a beaming grin across his face, Sam left the elevator at deck six. He had a twin cabin there on the uppermost crew deck. Usually reserved for married members of crew, such as Baker and Bhukari, he shared one with his grandmother. It had been refitted with two single beds instead of the usual double and I got the impression it suited them quite well.

I carried on up through the ship on my own, exiting the elevator when it finally reached the top deck. This time, when the elevator doors opened, a blast of sunshine hit me, stinging my eyes after the dimness of being below decks.

I blinked a few times as my eyes adjusted to the brightness. I hadn't carried my handbag this morning, it is not the sort of thing you really want when you're trying to catch criminals. Unless of course you wish to carry a house brick in it for walloping them, apparently.

I chuckled to myself at the memory as I made my way through the ship to get to my cabin. No handbag meant no key card to get inside. Although, since I'd gone for a dip, had I been carrying my key card it probably wouldn't have worked now anyway.

I knocked twice, rapping my knuckles smartly on the door, but I didn't get to tap a third time because the door opened inwards before I could.

'Madam,' Jermaine dipped his head, a small smile teasing the corners of his mouth to let me know he was pleased to see me and not even slightly shocked at the state I was now in.

Due to my relationship with that Maharaja I mentioned earlier, I was staying in the Windsor Suite, the finest suite on the entire ship, and one originally intended to be reserved for royalty. The suite came with a member of staff - a butler by the name of Jermaine Clarke. He saw to my every need, most usually anticipating what I wanted before I had the chance to ask for it. He possessed an uncanny sense for knowing when I was about to arrive at my door and must have had a team of spies employed because he generally knew what state I was going to arrive in, whether I had eaten, or if some problem had befallen me and would require his ear or possibly even a shoulder on which I could cry.

Jermaine was probably the best friend I had in the world, and I loved him most dearly.

My two dachshunds arrived at a sprint, barking all the way across the suite's main living space having leapt from the sofa on which they had been slumbering until my arrival. I got inside the door quickly so that Jermaine could shut it lest the two little monsters attempt an escape. They rather liked exploring the ship untethered.

'I have a bath run for you already, Madam, and a fresh selection of clothes laid out upon your bed. There is fresh coffee brewed and I have prepared a selection of breakfast items since you left here this morning before you had a chance to eat.'

I patted Jermaine's shoulder to show my thanks. The dogs were climbing my legs, their tiny claws scratching at my skin as they begged to be picked up. I didn't think it was a particularly good idea to scoop them for a hug given how sopping wet I still was. Besides, they would then find the ketchup, egg, and whatever else was stuck to me and start trying to lick it.

I shooed them back into the suite's main living area instead, tempting them with the promise of a biscuit.

'I placed a laundry hamper for wet items in the bathroom, Madam.' Jermaine let me know. He, of course, meant the private en suite bathroom in my bedroom. The Windsor Suite came with five bedrooms, two of which were currently occupied. One by me, and one by my other very good friend, Barbie.

Barbie spent as many nights in Hideki's accommodation as she did in mine. She wasn't in the suite now, but I knew where I could find her - in the top deck's exclusive gymnasium where she tortured people on a daily basis. I was one of those suckers who kept going back for more punishment because even though she was cruel and evil, she also knew her stuff, and I doubted I had been this fit or content with my body since I was in my very early twenties.

Telling myself I didn't need a workout today because I had already been for a swim – sort of true – I headed into my bedroom to get changed.

Less than half an hour after arriving back in my suite, I was sipping coffee in the kitchen and mentally preparing to go out again. I'd eaten a vegetable omelette that would keep me going for the rest of the morning and was keen to get going.

With the aim of wrapping things up as quickly as I could and hoping that Baker and the others had already got the bulk of the paperwork for the passport thieves done, I stuffed my phone into my handbag, collected the dogs from Jermaine, who was waiting at the door with the girls already clipped to the leads, and set off to find my team.

More than anything, I wanted to get ashore today. I had never been to Gibraltar, and Alistair, the captain of the ship who coincidentally also happens to be my boyfriend, had promised to show me a few things.

Setting out with a smile on my face, I had no idea how significant my trip ashore would prove to be.

Complaints

My phone rang before I was three yards from my suite. I withdrew it from my handbag expecting to see Alistair's name displayed – we were supposed to be heading into Gibraltar together after all and I hoped he was calling to confirm I was ready.

Seeing Hideki's name instead came as a surprise, but of course I answered it to see what he might want.

'Hi, Patricia,' he said with an apologetic tone. 'I'm sorry to have to do this so soon after the last dead body, but I'm afraid I've got another.'

My brow wrinkled, a mix of surprise and confusion messing with my face. Yet again, there had been no code word to alert the crew to the discovery of an unexpected dead passenger. To me this meant Hideki was telling me about a death from natural causes. We get those from time to time, and probably a higher percentage than another population might endure because we had quite a lot of elderly passengers who travelled with us.

'Is this a murder?' I asked. I could hear Hideki speaking to somebody at the other end, the muffled voice of another man saying something in the background.

Hideki did not, however, make me wait. 'No, Patricia, I don't think so.' I was about to ask why he was calling me, when he added, 'It's a little difficult to explain. Can you come to me?'

I had half a mind to say 'No,' and get on the phone to Baker and the team. If there was something fishy to be investigated, surely one of them could handle the initial gathering of data while I explored Gibraltar with Alistair. It was a plan that ticked all my boxes, but with a resigned sigh I asked the young doctor which cabin he was in and pointed my feet in that direction.

Anna and Georgie, my two miniature dachshunds didn't mind too much where we went. They were happy to go for a walk, tugging me along as they raced each other to get to wherever it was we were going. My decision to go myself was largely a matter of pride. I was still settling into the role as ship's detective, and felt I needed to prove myself. Or perhaps what I needed to prove was the necessity of the role.

Purple Star Lines was paying me handsomely, not that I needed it, but it felt good to earn my own money. It gave me a sense of independence and with that came freedom. If everything else in my life went wrong, I could support myself.

On my way to find Hideki and the latest passenger who would never see their destination, I called Alistair.

'Good morning, Patricia,' he answered the phone far more stiffly than he would normally and he used my name. He had several pet names he more frequently employed instead, including a couple reserved for the bedroom.

Reacting to the formality of his greeting, I asked, 'Is everything all right?'

I heard him sigh at the other end before he said, 'Yes. I guess. Hopefully.'

The jumbled-up sentence was a strange thing to hear from such an articulate man. Alistair was good with words - able to find the right thing to say in any given situation. It made him such an excellent choice as a cruise ship captain. I recognised that his was not an easy job, and he had many plates in the air which he needed to keep spinning at all times. The ship had a big crew giving Alistair many people to whom he could delegate. Ultimately though, like anyone in a position of responsibility, he internalised a lot of the pressure.

'Is this to do with the body on deck nineteen?' I asked, wondering if he was about to reveal some sordid mystery.

'What?' Alistair snapped out a surprised response. He didn't know anything about it. 'Has there been a murder?' he asked.

Giving him the most honest answer I could, I said, 'I'm not sure. Dr Nakamura asked me to meet him at the deceased passenger's cabin. He was a little cryptic about it. I'm on my way there now. I'm hoping to be able to wrap it up quickly, I still want to go into Gibraltar today,' I added hopefully. When Alistair did not respond immediately, a new thought occurred to me. 'Are you trying to let me know that you can't get away?' I asked.

Today would not be the first time that events transpired to thwart our plans for a nice day together. Expecting him to tell me that was precisely why he was calling and to be the reason why he had been struggling to find the right words to let me down, I was most shocked to learn that I was completely wrong.

'No, Patricia, it's not that at all. There's, um ... there's been some complaints,' he revealed.

'Complaints?' I echoed the word he employed. 'About you?' I was truly mystified. The captain was loved by the crew and popular with the passengers. I could not even conceive what someone would complain about.

'No, darling, the complaints are not about me,' he replied, a kind tone employed to sugar coat the bitter pill I was about to be asked to swallow.

Suddenly sensing what he was about to say, I felt an unexpected light headedness and a touch of nausea gripped me. 'The complaints are about you.'

The news was like a punch to my midriff, and I reeled from it. My feet stopped moving, the dachshunds tugging at my arm as they attempted to continue going. Finding a handy wall to lean against, I dipped my head a little, bending at the waist to get it below my heart.

'Someone complained about me,' I repeated, attempting to absorb the information. 'What did they complain about?'

'I'm afraid it's not just one complaint, darling. Actually, there's quite a few.' Alistair continued talking, words filling my ear though I barely heard them. Mostly I was concentrating on not throwing up. Where had I gone wrong? I believed I had been diligent in my duty as the ship's detective, assisting and in many ways leading Lieutenant Commander Baker and his team as we did our best to reduce crime on board the ship.

However, according to the captain, Purple Star Lines had been receiving complaints about me almost since I took up the post. The complaints were all from different people and he had taken the time to confirm they were all genuine passengers who had been onboard the ship. Alistair had been sitting on the complaints for more than a week, attempting to work out what to do about them while he conducted his own investigation to make sure they were not being generated by one person with a vendetta. The complaints ranged from being rude, to being threatening, and all the way up to forcing my way into someone's cabin because I believed they looked suspicious.

'But I haven't done that!' I protested. 'I haven't ever done anything like that,' I added, the volume of my voice rising with my righteous indignation.

I heard Alistair clear his throat. 'Well...'

I cut him off because I knew what he was about to say.

'Yes, yes, Alistair, but all the times I snuck into people's cabins in the past, I was merely a passenger on the ship. Now I'm a member of the crew. I can assure you, Captain, that at no point have I been rude or threatening. And I certainly haven't forced my way into anyone's cabin to accuse them of looking suspicious.'

Alistair didn't want to push me on the subject, or believed over the phone was not the right way to do it. What he said was, 'I am sure we can resolve this together, Patricia. Please do not allow this matter to spoil your day. I will be free to accompany you into Gibraltar when you're free to do so. But we must discuss this matter more fully before the sun sets.'

Feeling angry and trying to decide if that was an irrational reaction or not - I didn't think it was - I made sure to keep that negative emotion from my tone when I replied.

'That would be lovely, dear.'

He wished me luck in dealing with whatever awaited me on deck nineteen and promised to be waiting when I called to let him know I was ready to go ashore.

With a quick, 'Come along, girls,' I got my two Dachshunds moving again - they had taken the pause in forward motion as a cue to lie down for a nap. The nearest elevator was just around the corner, and empty when the doors opened. I descended to deck nineteen thinking about how my day was already going far from how I envisaged it might.

It was a good thing that I knew not to challenge it to get worse.

Cause of Death?

It was easy to spot the cabin I wanted by the white uniform standing outside it. Lieutenant Evermore spotted me coming, turning his head to announce me to the people inside the cabin before I arrived. I offered him a smile and held out my right hand, the one holding the two dog leads.

'Could you hold these for me?' I asked. 'I shouldn't be long.' The girls were already trying to get inside the cabin, curious to see whether there was any food inside probably. Evermore accepted the task of minding them and gave their lead a gentle tug to stop them going through the door after me.

Inside the cabin, I paused and looked about. There were two stewards standing to one side. They were not involved in proceedings yet, their presence required only so they could take the body away when Dr Nakamura released it.

There are a mix of cabin classes on deck nineteen, and this was one of the plusher suites. Significantly smaller than my own, it was nevertheless very nice and meant the person travelling in it had some money to spend. Some passengers would save up for years to take a cruise that would be referred to as the holiday of a lifetime. More commonly, those renting more expensive suites were well to do and hadn't needed to save at all.

To my right, a door led into the suite's bedroom from where my ears could detect the soft sound of someone walking on the carpet.

I called out, 'Hideki?'

He answered just as I got to the door, 'In the bedroom.'

'What have you got for me?' I asked, placing my handbag down on a dresser just inside the door. I had primed myself, expecting to find some terrible sight that might haunt me for days or months to come. To my surprise, the body in the room was in bed.

Curly white hair framed the friendly face of a woman in her late seventies. Though her cheeks were pale, she looked to be asleep. She was lying on her back with her shoulders and head above the covers and her arms lying on top of the sheets to either side of her body. Next to her on the nightstand was a pair of glasses, neatly folded and placed there ready for the morning. Next to them was a cup of water containing a set of dentures. And beyond that a photo frame that had been placed faced down.

I took all this in during the first few seconds, Hideki allowing me the time I needed to look around before speaking to me.

'She died of a heart attack so far as I can make out,' Hideki reported. 'I'll be able to confirm that easily enough when I get her to the medical centre. But since you are about to ask me why I would call you here for a woman who died of a heart attack, I should probably reveal that she has been posed.'

'Posed?' I queried, unsure that I understood him correctly.

Hideki stepped away from the body, joining me at the foot of the bed. With a nod of his head, he repeated himself.

'Yes, posed. She did not die in this position. People dying from a heart attack do not look like this. That's not all,' he added. 'There are signs that there was someone else in her bed last night.'

My eyes almost popped out on stalks.

'Is she travelling with her husband?'

Hideki shook his head. 'No, she's travelling with her sister. She's in the cabin next door. They are on their way to the Caribbean where they have family. Her passport is on the nightstand,' he pointed to it.

He would have used it to confirm who he was looking at and knew well enough that I would wish to confirm her identity too. She was British, I could tell by the colour of the passport, and was seventy-four years old – a touch younger than I had thought. I made a note of her name: Evelyn Rose Goodwin, and took a photograph of the passport in case I needed it.

'The sister is already aware?' I sought to confirm.

'She is the one who reported her sister's death,' Hideki replied solemnly. 'It seemed as if it came as quite a shock.'

My detective's brain was already working overtime, A queue of unruly questions fighting to be first in line to be asked.

I went with, 'What makes you think there was a man here last night?'

Hideki moved around the room, crossing in front of me to get to the other side of the bed where he pointed to something I had to squint at.

'There are strands of dark hair on the pillow, and I found more under the covers. They are cut short, as you can see.' I had to lean right in to confirm what he was telling me. 'It's a guess, but I would guess that Mrs Goodwin had a male guest in her bed last night.'

'You can confirm that?' I asked. 'Through DNA?'

'I can,' he nodded his head. 'I will need to add it to the list of things to do.'

With two bodies in a few hours, he probably had a glut of work to get through.

'Leave it for now – I might not need it confirmed, but please take samples and keep it in mind.' Pushing on, I asked, 'Could the sister be the one who posed Evelyn's body?'

Hideki shook his head. 'I don't think so. From the lady's temperature, I would estimate that she died before midnight last night. She would need to have been posed like this quite quickly after she passed away otherwise rigour mortis would have set in and made it impossible. Unless her sister decided to sit on the news for the last ten hours, it could not have been her.'

Clearly, I was going to have to talk to the deceased's next of kin. But for the time being I was trying to work out what it was that I was investigating. The lady being posed, if it wasn't her sister, was suspicious for sure. But if Hideki could prove that the lady had died from a heart attack, then it wasn't murder. So what was it?

I looked about, searching for clues. And while doing so, I removed my phone from my handbag.

'Lieutenant Commander Baker,' Martin answered his phone formally even though he must have known it was me at the other end. 'Are you ashore yet, Mrs Fisher? I don't think we need you for anything at the moment if you're just checking in. There's some paperwork to sign but that can be taken care of later.'

I blew out a small sigh of exasperation, questioning how much of my day this was going to eat up, then got on with the task of explaining why I was calling.

'Do you want me to bring Ensign Chalk with me?' he asked once I was done.

Though I knew Sam would cancel his plans to help me with the case - it was his job after all - he had been working without a break for several days and I knew he was looking forward to some shore time.

With a shake of my head that Baker couldn't see, I replied, 'No. There's no need.'

Baker let me know he was taking Schneider with him to hand off the passport thieves to the local police and sending Lieutenants Bhukari and Pippin to deck nineteen to assist me.

By the time they arrived, most of the passengers had disembarked. Through the window of Evelyn's suite, I could see them moving away from the ship, some on foot, others taking taxis or the Purple Star Lines limousines. They were off to enjoy themselves, exploring and eating, or maybe just relaxing. It was exactly what I had planned for my day and a vast contrast to what I was doing.

Distracting myself so I wouldn't be tempted to wallow, I left Evelyn's suite to speak with her sister. Priscilla Purcell, also a widow, had not expected her younger sister to be the first to go. She certainly hadn't expected to lose her on this trip.

I learned that Evelyn had been married for fifty years and had four children. Her husband, Teddy, had died five years ago right before his seventy-third birthday. It left Evelyn alone and confused after spending almost every day with the same person since they married when she was just nineteen. Priscilla lost her husband the same year.

While Bhukari and Pippin dismantled Evelyn's life, looking for clues as we did our best to ensure there was either no crime to investigate or that we were hard on the heels of a criminal if there was one, I was sipping tea in Priscilla's cabin.

The tea was my idea – something to keep Priscilla occupied in her bereavement and to distract her while I carefully picked at her brains. The dachshunds had entertained Priscilla briefly, their naturally inquisitive natures demanding they roam and explore until I called them back to settle next to my chair.

'What did Evelyn do last night?' I asked, sipping at my hot beverage with my pinky finger extended.

Priscilla picked up her cup and took a sip of the hot liquid, her eyes darting nervously about as she sought to look anywhere but at me. I have been investigating crimes for less than a year, but it was long enough for me to understand that I was seeing a furtive gesture.

'Um, we went out for some dinner,' Priscilla supplied an answer just before I needed to prompt one.

Firing off my next question immediately, I asked, 'Where did you go?' I was attempting to establish if Priscilla was making things up as she went along. It would be relatively easy to check if she was lying. It wasn't so much that I was suspicious of her having a hand in her sister's death – if Hideki was right, she died of natural causes, but someone posed Evelyn and that required some explanation. Combined with the nervous and secretive way Priscilla was acting, I believed there was something going on and I would not be satisfied until I was able to uncover what it was.

'La Trattoria,' Priscilla replied without needing to think. That much was true then, she had eaten at the Italian restaurant on board the ship. It was one of my favourites too. It didn't mean that the sisters had eaten together though.

'Ooh, I love that place,' I remarked with a wistful smile. 'They serve the best tiramisu. What did you have last night?'

I had her talking, and that made it far more likely that I would walk her into a lie that I could then catch her in. If I could do that, and she knew she had been caught, it would be relatively easy to then force her to tell the truth about whatever was going on.

Fielding the easy question, Priscilla said, 'I had a rather nice squid ink pasta served with fresh calamari and clams. The sauce was a little spicy, but I really rather enjoyed it.'

Casually, I asked my next question, 'What did your sister have? I guess it was her last meal and that's something to be remembered.'

Again, Priscilla fielded the question without needing to think. I had been watching her eyes, to see if they would go up and left to engage the imagination portion of her brain. Few people are aware that they do this when they decide to lie. It is a great tool for a detective to learn and employ, of course it only works when the person being interviewed is unaware. Cagier characters will know to move their eyes differently, throwing the person questioning them off the trail.

I learned that Evelyn had eaten a hearty portion of a vegetarian gnocchi dish. Priscilla said it in such a way that made me think she did not approve of vegetarians in general. I did not inquire as to her sister's dietary habits; they did not seem pertinent.

My initial belief that Priscilla was trying to hide something stayed with me, but I was not asking the right questions.

Trying a new approach, I asked, 'There's a lot of rather nice, older gentlemen around, did you two ladies attract any attention since you came on board?' I said it with a cheeky twinkle in my eye, trying to make it sound as if I was just making conversation. Priscilla deserved to have someone to keep her company in this awful time, but I was also providing her with an opportunity to reveal that her sister had met someone.

Priscilla reacted as if I had just insulted her, or her sister's memory perhaps. Glaring at me as she put her cup and saucer on a side table, she said, 'I think you ought to leave now, Mrs Fisher. You've outstayed your welcome.'

I didn't move, except to lift my cup to take another sip of tea while I observed her. I had not expected to find myself at this point in the conversation so swiftly. In fact, I hadn't really expected to find myself at this point at all. I expected to discover that Evelyn had indeed met a gentleman, and that she had died last night, hopefully in the throes of ecstasy.

My guess was that the gentleman had then informed Priscilla and between the two of them they had made Evelyn look peaceful and respectful, agreeing on a plan to reveal Evelyn's death of natural causes in the morning.

Instead, I had unwittingly uncovered something else.

'I asked you to go, Mrs Fisher,' Priscilla repeated her request, adding, 'Must I call security?'

I took my time, carefully placing my cup back on its saucer now that I had drained it of tea, then placed them both on a table to the side of my chair.

Locking eyes with Priscilla I said, 'Security on this ship work with me. I have two of them next door right now, going through your sister's things as we attempt to establish what happened to her. The doctor who examined her and confirmed that she had passed, was able to easily determine that she had been posed. He is yet to confirm it, but he believes she had a man in her bed last night.'

Priscilla had her mouth open slightly, possibly wanting to deny what I was saying, or argue, but I didn't give her the chance.

'I consider it to be a matter of professional responsibility to know when a person is lying to me, Priscilla. And you just did. Whatever it is that you know about the circumstances of your sister's death, you should tell me now. Tell me who the man was, Priscilla. Did he pose her, or did you? Or was it a combined effort?' Accusation delivered, I fell silent, watching her to see what her face might do in reaction to my words.

She looked shocked, but then she ought to anyway because her sister died unexpectedly last night. Her hands were nervously fiddling with each other, held in her lap as she sat with her knees together perched on the edge of her armchair. I had made her uncomfortable, as was my intention, but she did not fold and give me the answers I wanted as I had hoped she might.

Flicking her head up so her eyes were no longer boring into the carpet, she met my gaze.

'I have no idea what you are talking about, Mrs Fisher. I found my sister this morning, letting myself into her room with the spare key card she gave me when she failed to answer the text message I sent her. You can check my phone if you wish, it was just after eight o'clock. I was checking to make sure that she was up and about because I was getting hungry and wanted breakfast.'

Changing tack, as a thought occurred to me, I asked, 'Are you being blackmailed? Is there someone on this ship who you need protection from? We can do that,' I assured her. 'There's no need to worry. If you think your sister was murdered, you can tell me.'

'My sister died in her sleep, Mrs Fisher. Good luck proving otherwise.'

I pressed her a little harder, but I was consciously holding back for one very simple reason – the complaints. If Priscilla was innocent – I hadn't figured out if there even was a crime yet – then bullying her hours after a bereavement would not be well received if it found its way to the ears of those in Purple Star HQ.

Either way, she wasn't budging from her story, so I was going to have to gather the evidence to prove what lie she was telling.

I left Priscilla in her suite shortly thereafter. Lieutenant Bhukari confiscated her passport upon my instruction. Priscilla could go where she pleased on board the ship, but I did not want her going ashore and vanishing. Not until I had worked out what it was that I was investigating.

Was it a clever murder? If so, what was the motive and who was the killer?

The deceased's sister was hiding something, that much I knew for sure. But I had no idea what it was. If she was guilty, then she had an accomplice - the mysterious man who spent the night with Evelyn and was most likely with her in her final moments.

I read in a detective novel once that the last person to see a victim alive is always the killer. So now it came down to Hideki establishing just how Mrs Goodwin had died.

Was it murder or not?

Sapphire of Fate

It was close to lunch and my stomach was rumbling by the time I made it ashore with Alistair. First on our agenda had to be a restaurant. Fortunately, there were many places offering wonderful food from which we could pick.

So close to Spain, it was no shock when we found a delightful looking Spanish taverna. It had a wonderful view over the ocean, the sun dancing on the wave tips where it hung from an azure blue sky.

We ordered paella, a large platter of it to go in the middle of the table for us to share. It was every bit as wonderful as I imagined it might be. It was so tasty, in fact, that I found myself in a race to get halfway across the platter before Alistair could begin to gobble up any of my half. By the time I finished, I knew I had eaten more than I needed, but could not feel bad about it. Patting my bloated stomach, I felt glad we had nothing more strenuous than a little shopping planned for our afternoon.

Alistair and I had been an item for several months now. One could say it had been a little on and off, I guess, because I left the ship for more than two months as I tried to find out who I was. At fifty-three, my life changed dramatically as I went from bored housewife to lady with money and independence. Standing on my own two feet for the first time in my life, I could not move straight from one relationship to another. Not even for someone as handsome and promising as Alistair.

So I fought against my emotions, giving into them only when circumstance reunited us. All doubt had since been cast from my mind to the point that I had stopped thinking 'I' and 'me' and begun considering things in terms of 'us' and 'we'.

He still lived in the captain's quarters, high up on the bridge superstructure where he had easy access to all that was important in managing the ship. We would visit each other's accommodation, spending what time together we could afford, and there was rarely anything either one of us considered doing that would not involve the other unless it was work.

Our lunch conversation skirted around the very obvious subject of the complaints filed against me. It sat like an uncomfortable elephant in the room, but we had agreed to leave it until later so that we could enjoy our time together first.

When we were finished with our lunch, and I had a little buzz going from the large glass of pinot grigio I'd consumed, we strolled arm in arm through the streets of Gibraltar Town. We had no agenda, other than to spend some time together. There was nothing in particular that we needed, but we entertained ourselves with a little bit of window shopping, soaking up the sights and sounds of the odd little British territory tacked on to the end of Spain.

I knew very little about the history of the island, but as usual, as if he were a tour guide rather than a cruise ship captain, Alistair proved to be full of information. He talked and I listened, basking in the afternoon sun, and feeling thoroughly content.

Drifting along, I was paying little attention to what I was looking at until my eyes caught upon something in the window of a jewellery store. I might not have noticed it at all, had a man inside the shop not been rearranging the display at the time.

Right in the centre of his window, between displays of rings and watches, he was arranging a beautiful necklace. As he moved it into position, the jewel caught the sun and the large stone set into the pendant dazzled me momentarily.

The man inside the window leaned to one side to better inspect his display and make sure the necklace was hanging evenly. I had stopped moving, drawing Alistair to a halt too, and now he was following my gaze to see what I was looking at.

'Now that, my dear, has Patricia Fisher written all over it,' Alistair commented with a snort of amusement.

The man inside the shop, the proprietor, I assumed, reacted as a person does when they suddenly realise someone is watching them. Looking up, he saw a middle-aged couple standing arm in arm and looking at the object he had just placed on display.

It felt like one of those fateful moments, when the stars align, or whatever it is that astrologists say. Whatever it was, I was looking at a necklace that held a large blue sapphire. It was the exact same shape as the one I returned to the Maharaja of Zangrabar, and it was speaking to me.

Mostly, it was saying, 'Buy me, I'm really, really pretty.'

Drawn as if by a magnet, I found myself making my way inside the jeweller's shop. The man was no longer in the window, and neither was the necklace. It was displayed around a cut-off mannequin's neck to demonstrate how it might look when worn, and the jeweller - professional you-can-trust-me smile in place - was placing it on a glass topped counter so that we could inspect it more closely.

'You should try it on, darling,' Alistair suggested, flicking his eyebrows at the jeweller who seemed only too pleased to assist.

In seconds, the clasp was undone, and it was in Alistair's hands, my boyfriend manoeuvring behind me as I held my hair out of the way so that he could connect the two ends once more.

'Exquisite,' the jeweller remarked, clapping his hands together joyfully. His accent was British, but with a slight Spanish lilt. He was heavily tanned, and though probably of British descent, I would not be surprised to learn that he had lived in Gibraltar his entire life. He was saying all the right things if he wanted to make a sale, but I already knew I was going to buy it before I stepped inside his shop.

To my surprise, I was wrong.

'Will you allow me to buy it for you, darling?' Alistair enquired.

I had not seen a price tag, and Alistair had not enquired what the item of jewellery might cost. I for one had not the faintest idea what a sapphire like this might be worth.

Feeling a little off balance, I said, 'How much is it, please?'

The jeweller opened his mouth to reply, but was cut off swiftly by Alistair.

'Please do not advise the lady regarding the price until she has answered my question, sir.'

The jeweller dutifully dipped his head in response and remained quiet while both men waited for me to reply to Alistair's request.

Narrowing my eyes at the handsome captain for a moment I tried a different question, 'Can you tell me how many carats the stone is, please?'

The jeweller did not answer me immediately, he shifted his eyes to check with Alistair first. The two men were ganging up on me.

Getting a nod from my boyfriend, the jeweller announced, 'It's a little over five carats, Madam.'

Getting an answer didn't actually provide me with any information – I had no idea what five carats would mean the stone was worth. I was, however, willing to place the value between 'quite a bit', and 'really rather a lot' of money. I could look it up later, but right now I was stuck with a tough choice. I was just getting used to being an independent woman with her own money and able to stand on her own two feet, and here I had the debonair captain attempting to pay for things that I wanted to buy for myself.

Was I harming my independence if I allowed him to make the purchase? Would I insult him if I refused to let him buy me what was essentially a trinket?

I flipped a mental coin, watched how it landed, and offered Alistair a sweet smile.

'If you truly wish to spend your money in such a manner, my dear, then I will not prevent you.'

A few minutes later we were meandering back towards the ship because we had spotted a bar there earlier. Stopping for a drink would allow us to watch the waves and chat about whatever subjects took our fancy. Dangling from my left hand, as my right was interwoven with Alistair's left, was my handbag with the fancy, and undoubtedly expensive, sapphire necklace inside it.

The jeweller had placed it neatly into a case, a degree of pomp and ceremony employed in so doing as if it were part of the experience to watch his flourishing motions. I kept quiet and let him do it, though honestly, I quite fancied just putting it on and waltzing up the Aurelia's boarding ramp with it around my neck.

It was, of course, not a casual piece of jewellery for everyday wear. It was, however, something I could easily get away with wearing at any of the regular balls that took place on board the ship.

We were about halfway to the bar when my phone rang. I wasn't expecting anyone to call me, which is to say that I was hoping to be left alone and knew that all the people who knew me would be kind enough to do so unless they had good reason not to.

The name displayed on my screen when I fished the phone from my handbag, was that of Deepa Bhukari. Guessing that it had to do with one of the two bodies found today, I let go of Alistair's arm and thumbed the green button to answer the call.

'Hi, Deepa, did something turn up?' I asked.

She wasted no time on small talk, the former Pakistani infantry soldier getting straight to the point.

'We found an ATM receipt from one of the onboard cash dispensers in Mrs Goodwin's handbag. She withdrew five hundred dollars in cash last night and there is no sign of it anywhere now.'

'So she was robbed,' I jumped to what I felt was a natural conclusion. We had gone from death by natural causes under slightly suspicious circumstances to a robbery that had gone horribly wrong. Was posing her part of an attempt to cover up what had happened?

'Well, that's the strange thing, Mrs Fisher,' Deepa commented. 'There *was* money in her purse, eighty-three dollars to be exact. Her safe wasn't locked and there was money in there too. Plus, she had jewellery in her cabin - items that would be relatively easy to sell.'

I wasn't sure what to make of it. Five hundred dollars in cash was not a small amount to go missing. I wasn't going to question whether Deepa had been thorough in her search of the cabin because I knew she would have been, especially when she discovered there was something to look for.

'She might have used it to purchase something?' I hazarded, throwing an idea at Deepa even though I was certain she would have already thought of that.

'It's something we're looking into,' she replied, sounding distracted as if she were thinking of something while she was talking to me. 'I tried to ask the sister about it. You spoke to her this morning didn't you, Mrs Fisher? Did you get any sense that she was being evasive?'

I pulled a face that was aimed at myself, glad that it wasn't just me who had noticed it.

'Yes, I asked whether Evelyn might have made a romantic connection during her time on the Aurelia, and she demanded that I leave her cabin. It was a strange reaction and completely disproportionate. There is something going on here, but I have no idea what it is.'

'Well, I'm afraid that's not the only reason for my call, Mrs Fisher. We've got another case to look into on top of this one,' Deepa announced.

'Don't tell me there's a third dead body,' I closed my eyes and prayed that would not be the case.

My response drew a snigger from the young woman at the other end.

'Nothing so grand, I'm afraid. It looks like we have another case of honey trap theft. There's a family staying in the Platinum Suite.' I knew this to be one of the largest suites on the ship. 'The case has been reported by Tim Oswald, who believes his father, the billionaire head of the Oswald Corporation, is being led on a merry dance by a rather attractive young lady who is stealing things each time she visits the suite. He wants us to deal with the matter delicately because he worries his elderly father – he's eighty-two – might not react well if he – Mr Tim Oswald – accuses the young woman directly. I believe he wants us to collect evidence and prove the case first.'

'Do we know the identity and circumstances of the lady he is pointing a finger at?'

I heard Deepa tapping at her tablet to bring up the information.

'Betty Ross, single, aged twenty-two.'

I whistled – it was a considerable age gap.

'That was my reaction too,' Deepa admitted when she heard me. 'She was travelling with friends, but they all left the ship in Marrakesh. I believe Mr Oswald Senior is now picking up her bills which is how she has remained onboard.'

Deepa was right that this was another case – we could hardly ignore it. That they were staying in the Platinum Suite indicated the Oswalds were really rather rich, but like most cruise ships, the Aurelia catered to people of all budgets. This strategy put multimillionaires mere yards away from people with just enough money to save up for a once in a lifetime short cruise staying in one of the lower-level cabins.

Consequently, there were men and women who came aboard hoping they might meet someone who would change their circumstances. Of course, not all age-gap romances were untoward or wrong. Love can be such a strange and fickle thing.

Yes, I felt the age gap between the two persons was quite extreme - surely, they would have few things in common and it must be difficult to come up with shared life experiences to discuss. However, I would not allow myself to condemn something out of hand just because I did not understand it.

'So Mr Oswald Junior would like us to find the evidence to prove the young lady in question is stealing from them?' I wanted to make sure I had it right in my head.

'That's about it, yes,' agreed Deepa. 'He seems really quite upset about it all.'

'Anything else?' I offered her the chance to give me all the bad news at once.

'Um, is the captain there?'

I flicked my eyes to where Alistair was inspecting a stand of hats. He was killing time while he waited for me to finish my call.

'He is,' I replied. 'Do you need to speak with him?'

'Ooh, no thanks,' Deepa sucked a breath between her teeth. 'You might want to let him know that we have a minor problem with some monkeys though, just to prepare him for the drama when he returns.'

'Monkeys?' I wasn't sure I had heard her right.

'Well, Gibraltar Rock Apes to be precise. This is not the first time this has happened, apparently.'

'Righto, I'll let him know. Listen, I think we need to take a close look at Evelyn's sister. There was something very off about her as you already said. I think she's the one who posed Evelyn to make her look like she died peacefully in her sleep – that's not a crime per se, and if she is the one who took the five hundred dollars, that's not really something we can charge her with either. There is something screwy going on though. She pretty much challenged me to prove her sister didn't die in her sleep.'

'Why would she do that?' Deepa replied in a mystified tone.

I had no idea. Yet. So I said, 'Exactly. We need to have a look in her suite, examine her finances as best we can, see if there is a reason why she would want her sister dead, and maybe do a little switcharoo with her handbag.' It was a firm belief of mine that if a person was concerned about others finding a piece of evidence that they could not destroy or discard, then they kept it about their person. In the case of a lady, such as Priscilla, that would mean in her handbag.

'I didn't just overhear you suggesting you were going to steal a passenger's handbag, did I, darling?' Alistair asked in an innocent voice.

'No,' I lied impulsively. 'You misheard me because there is so much background noise here.'

He cocked his head to listen for a second – it was so quiet I would be able to hear if a nearby fish had digestive problems.

'Is that the captain?' asked Deepa while my cheeks coloured. 'Don't forget to tell him about the monkeys.'

I promised I would do precisely that though I wasn't sure what the fuss was about. There were a couple of monkeys on board - it didn't sound like a particularly big deal to me.

Alistair uttered some particularly unpleasant words when I let him know.

'Every time we come to Gibraltar, we get the same problem. It wouldn't be so bad if other cruise ships suffered as well. But there's something about the Aurelia and they remember us.'

'Do they cause a problem?' I was curious to hear why he was so upset.

Alistair was punching himself in the head, his left fist banging against his left temple.

'They terrorise the passengers for a start and they're so difficult to get rid of. We were halfway across the Atlantic last year when we finally caught the last one. To add insult to injury, Purple Star then had to pay to ship them all back to Gibraltar.'

Now, I don't know why I let my mouth do this to me but before I knew what was happening, I was volunteering to deal with it for him. Perhaps it was that he just spent a silly amount of money on a necklace for me. Perhaps it was because I knew I was falling in love with him, and I hated to see the stress he felt rising to the surface. It was so rare for him to willingly reveal that something troubled him, but whatever it was that drove me to do it, once the words were out of my mouth, I couldn't take them back.

'Really?' he replied, his fist dropping back to his side as he looked at me with hope. 'I guess the ship has never had someone like you to take on a task like this. You've got your team, of course,' he remarked, as if suddenly remembering them. 'This will be so much better than it sucking up everyone else's time.'

He stuck out his elbow for me to loop my arm through and started walking once more.

I already had three cases to investigate, plus the ridiculous complaints levied against me to deal with yet. Adding the task of rounding up a bunch of Gibraltar Rock Apes to the list was not a wise move on my part. However, I wasn't going to start complaining about my burden.

Not yet. That would come later when I realised what I had let myself in for.

Whodunit?

In the little bar by the water, Alistair settled me at a table and went to the bar.

'Cooee!'

The raucous call echoed across the bar, two dozen patrons inside the establishment turning their heads to see who had made the noise. I didn't need to look, I already knew.

I hadn't noticed her when we came in, but had I done so, I would not have started walking in the opposite direction. For though Gloria Chalk was a bit of a handful, and an acquired taste, she was also to be found with one of my favourite people on the planet.

Turning around to spot where she was, I found my assistant, Sam, waving at me in his usual jovial manner.

'Hello, Mrs Fisher.' Just like his grandmother, he raised his voice so he could be heard all the way across the bar.

Accepting the inevitable, I abandoned the table for two I had chosen by the water and walked my dachshunds across to where the Chalks were sitting.

Sam had been forced to leave his own puppy behind when he agreed to take the post on the Aurelia. It was a tough compromise for him to make, but crew were not permitted pets – it just wasn't a safe environment for them to be kept in, most especially a dog.

His parents were happily looking after it until he returned. Like everyone else in every other job around the world, he would get time off and could return home if he chose to at that point. He would find his dog waiting, but until then he was happy to entertain Anna and Georgie who powered across the ground to get to him.

'Have you had a good day, Sam?' I asked him after I'd greeted Gloria with a quick air kiss.

'There are monkeys on the boat!' Sam laughed in response to my question, the news far too exciting to actually provide me with an answer.

I nodded. 'Yes, so I've heard. Actually, I have a little bit of news on that subject. We're going to be heading up the task of getting the monkeys off the ship again.'

Sam tipped back his head to whoop his excitement - he sure was fun to be around. Just as the list of all the things I needed to do was beginning to get me down, there was Sam to buoy me back up.

Laughing along with him, I took a couple of moments to tell him about the other cases we had to investigate.

Gloria had a question for me, and had been attempting to pose it ever since I sat down.

'Is that nice feller of yours buying drinks?' she asked with only the barest attempt at subtlety.

I glanced across at the bar where I could see there were more glasses being placed on a tray than he and I were going to drink. He had seen me move tables and knew well enough what Gloria would want.

Satisfied that her empty glass was going to be refreshed, she had something else to say.

'Sam tells me there was a body found down deep in the hold this morning.'

'He was murdered,' Sam chipped in, not wanting that important detail to be overlooked.

'Any clues as to who done it?' Gloria wanted to know, looking for some juicy gossip to spread amongst the small circle of friends she had already made on board.

I shook my head. 'No, it's far too early to tell. He's been dead for a while and might have been a stowaway. My team and I will conduct the investigation, but I don't hold out a lot of hope when it comes to catching his killer.'

Alistair arrived with our drinks, and the conversation rolled on. Gibraltar isn't a particularly big place, though it is a nice one for people to visit and the cruise ships often stop there on their way in or out of the Mediterranean. When the sun set tonight, the passengers would all come back on board and the Aurelia would once again get on her way.

It was one of the greatest joys of living and working aboard a cruise ship - almost every day heralded a new location and thus a new adventure.

Just as the sun began to dip toward the horizon, we finished our drinks and made our way back to the ship.

Little did I know I was being watched.

Monkey Business

I had it in my head that there were some apes on board but the picture my imagination concocted was nothing like what was waiting to greet us when we returned to the Aurelia.

Alistair muttered something that could not be repeated in church, but his comment was warranted - we could all see the debacle taking place in front of us.

Passengers were returning to the ship, but they were doing so amid a mass of crew who were attempting to drive back yet more Gibraltar Rock Apes. The apes – bigger than I had realised – were running rings around the crew, charging up the gangplanks and climbing the ropes and chains that held the ship against the quayside.

This was in addition to the crew on the ship trying to get rid of the rock apes who were already onboard. There were white uniforms dashing here and there, many of them were carrying bats or wooden brooms, or some other implement they could use to herd the acrobatic primates.

In general, they were not doing very well, and passengers were squawking in shock or surprise, and jumping out of the way as an apologetic member of crew ran past them trying to chase yet another monkey back toward the island.

At ground level, Anna and Georgie were going nuts. They could see something to chase and that was precisely what they wanted to do. If I were to let them off their leads, I might never see them again.

Alistair let go my hand and began running, but he only got two paces before he stopped himself. Turning around, he came back to my side to kiss me tenderly on my left cheek.

'Good luck dealing with this, darling. I do hope I'll see you a little later for some dinner. Perhaps we can discuss that other matter,' I knew that he meant the complaints levied against me, 'and get that put to bed before we...' he shot me a cheeky grin, 'Get to bed.'

Without giving me the opportunity to respond, he quickly darted away, calling loudly, 'Captain coming through. Make way please.' The crowd swallowed him, the dirty rotter leaving me to deal with the mess I foolishly volunteered to tackle.

Sam was loving the display, chortling merrily as he watched the primates easily evading the harassed looking crew.

'Coo, this is a fine to do,' Gloria observed, drastically understating the issue.

Muttering under my breath I said, 'Yes, and it's my to do to undo.'

I didn't bother trying to explain how I got to the point where I was supposed to be dealing with the mess, instead I went around the crowd of passengers filing into the ship's main entrance to get to the royal suites' entrance near the prow of the ship.

I could have used the crew entrance, but I worried Alistair might have already informed the crew manning it that I was going to be heading up the monkey removal effort. I wanted to change my clothes before they begged me to take over and coordinate their efforts. I rather liked the outfit I'd chosen today and had no desire to see it destroyed chasing Gibraltar Rock Apes off the ship.

Also, I needed a few moments to think the problem through and devise a solution that could tackle the problem holistically, rather than what I was witnessing now which was the crew chasing the rock apes individually.

Lieutenants Sean and Collins were manning the royal suites' entrance today - both gave me a smile and nod of greeting as they welcomed me back to the ship. I took Gloria and Sam with me, making their access to the ship a simpler affair too. I am quite unique among the crew on board the ship in that I tread the line somehow between passenger and crew member. Unlike all the other crew I do not have a rank, I am employed as the ship's detective though at the same time I'm nominally in charge of Lieutenant Commander Baker's team. Dating the captain ensures that I am very well known, but I am also the passenger staying in the ship's most luxurious suite, and that alone would otherwise ensure that I was accorded the greatest of care and respect by all crew members.

Just inside the ship, an elevator was waiting to whisk us up to the top floors. Sam and Gloria made to get out on deck seven so they could then backtrack to a crew elevator - the only way to get to their accommodation on deck six from where we were. As he attempted to move forward, I grabbed Sam's shoulder.

'Where do you think you're going, Sam?' I inquired. 'We have several investigations to conduct, and a monkey problem to which we must attend. You're coming with me Ensign Chalk.'

Sam was fine with that, a broad grin crossing his face as he waved his granny goodbye. Gloria tottered off down the passageway, vanishing from sight as the elevator doors swished together once more.

'Do I need to be in uniform, Mrs Fisher?' Sam asked.

My assistant was dressed casually in shorts and a t-shirt displaying a dinosaur motif. I didn't think it mattered one bit. Besides, his uniform was the same pure brilliant white as the rest of the security team, and I had seen several of them chasing the monkeys while sporting suspiciously brown marks on their usually immaculate clothes.

I pushed that thought from my mind as I reached the door to my suite and it opened in front of me before I could find my key card.

'Good afternoon, madam,' Jermaine greeted me, his extended hand waiting to take the dog leads.

'Hello, Jermaine,' I replied, forcing joviality into my voice rather than embrace the dread I was beginning to feel over the first task on my 'To Do' list.

As I made my way to the bedroom, from the corner of my eye I caught my Butler and my assistant performing a complicated, multistage hand shaking routine. Jermaine was an absolute treasure, adding joy to so many parts of my life already, so it came as no surprise that he had fully embraced my assistant's limited mental age. Jermaine handled Sam appropriately, dropping his stiff (fake) Britishness whenever Sam was around.

A few minutes later, I emerged from my bedroom wearing a pair of jeans, my rattiest pair of running shoes, and a long sleeve t-shirt. My hair was pulled back into a tight ponytail, and I had a ball cap on my head, just in case.

My phone rang, interrupting my thoughts. I went to my handbag to retrieve it.

For the third or possibly fourth time today, Dr Hideki Nakamura was calling me. I felt a small twitch of uneasiness in my core, and attempted to quash it as I told myself he would be calling about one of the current dead bodies, not another new one.

Mercifully, I was right.

'It's about our stowaway, Patricia,' Hideki informed me. 'I've, err ... I've found something in his stomach.'

I waited a second, expecting him to reveal a little more, and when he didn't, I prompted him.

'Can you be a little bit more specific, Hideki?'

I heard him suck a little air between his teeth before he answered.

'Treasure. I've found treasure in the stowaway's stomach. It looks like uncut gemstones. Quite a few of them, actually.'

I found my face scrunching itself up as I squinted in confusion.

'Treasure?' I knew that I had heard correctly but couldn't help myself from repeating the word he had employed. 'The man looked like he didn't have a penny to his name,' I remarked, remembering the threadbare nature of his clothes and the emaciated state of his body. 'What on earth would he be doing with uncut gemstones in his gut?'

Hideki chuckled; his mirth an emotion that did not seem to be appropriate in the present situation.

'I'm afraid, Patricia, that's where you come in,' he replied, explaining what had amused him. 'Solving mysteries is your department.'

Well, he made a fair point there. I had a mysterious dead person who may or may not be a stowaway, but who had not been reported as missing at any point in the last months or more. Whether he was a passenger or not, he had almost certainly been murdered, and now I had a potential motive for it. I would have to go and see the body again, and more pertinently, the gemstones when I had a chance later today. I had to admit that it was tweaking my interest.

Promising to get to him as soon as I could, I excused myself because I knew I had more pressing issues to deal with at this time.

The moment I hung up, I found both Jermaine and Sam staring at me with wide eyes and interested expressions.

'Treasure?' asked Sam. 'Like ... pirates?'

A smile filled my face, triggered by the boyish excitement contained within his eyes. That my own staid butler looked almost as excited as my assistant came as a surprise but was even more amusing.

'Nobody said pirates,' I pointed out. 'But, if you must know, Dr Hideki has found what he believes to be uncut gemstones in the stomach of the man we found in the hold this morning.'

'The stowaway, madam?' Jermaine wanted to confirm what he knew thus far.

'Yes,' I nodded. 'I'm afraid you'll have to excuse us; Sam and I need to tackle a rather worrying problem on deck.'

I hadn't noticed as I hurried to my suite to get changed, but going back into the passageway outside now, I could see through the windows that the top deck sun lounge had been abandoned. On a sunny day, such as it was today, it ought to be overflowing with happy people in swimsuits. They would be drinking cocktails, reading books, and generally soaking up the sunshine. Instead, there was nobody.

Or so I thought at first.

As I watched from the safety of the passageway overlooking the pool, a pair of Gibraltar Rock Apes leapt from the structure above me to land on a table and from that bounced down onto the deck. A second later, and coming from three different directions, three crew members charged after the apes. They were screaming banshee cries and attempting to herd the invading primates towards the edge of the ship. One carried a net, the other two had paddles, presumably taken from the water sports store.

Observing the fruitless, yet hard effort of the crew attempting to round up the apes, I devised a new plan. With Sam on my heels, I strode out onto the deck and shouted for the crew members to stop what they were doing.

All three screeched to a halt, turning to face me so that I at least got to see who it was now. They were out of breath, two stewards and one member of the security team. I didn't know the steward's names, but the security officer was one I had spoken to many times.

Addressing him, I said, 'Lieutenant Kashmir, the captain has been generous enough to place me in charge of this round up effort. Do you have your radio with you?' I asked.

He did, of course, happily crossing the deck at a more sedate pace to hand it to me.

I had gotten used to carrying one of the security team radios since I took up my post as ship's detective, and would need to replace the one I took for a swim as soon as possible. Opening a channel, I addressed as many of the crew as would be carrying radios.

'This is Patricia Fisher addressing all crew members engaged in the attempt to round up the Gibraltar Rock Apes. Please all desist. Stop your current activity and meet me on deck six outside storeroom four.' Then, remembering correct radio procedure, I clicked the send switch again, to add, 'Patricia out.'

Lieutenant Kashmir and the two stewards were regaining their breath and looked thoroughly pleased at my instruction to stop chasing the infernal primates. However, the security officer had a question for me.

'Mrs Fisher, what is it that we're doing on deck six? What's in storeroom four?'

I shot him what I hoped was a knowing smile and wiggled my eyebrows at him.

'You'll see soon enough,' I replied cryptically.

I rather think I would have come across as clever and enigmatic had it not been for the monkey poop striking the front of my shirt in the very next second.

Sam, Lieutenant Kashmir, and the two stewards darted back a yard to get away from me and twisted around to look up at the raised structure above us. We were on the top deck, but helicopter platforms and places to view and sunbathe existed above us. Spinning around to see where the poop had come from, a horrified expression on my face, I found a row of about a dozen of the rock apes staring down at me.

My disbelief trebled when one of them lifted its right hand and extended its middle finger in my direction.

I couldn't believe it! It's one thing to have to deal with the monkeys and their poop flinging, but this was adding insult to injury. What next, would they start writing letters of complaint about me?

Though it made no sense to do so, I began telling the primates off.

'How dare you? What is wrong with you that you feel the need to throw poop at people?'

My question of course was answered by several of the shaggy brown primates reaching one hand behind themselves.

I screamed and ran for it!

The stewards, Lieutenant Kashmir, and Sam were all ahead of me, already showing me their heels as they ran to get away from the primates and their mucky missiles.

I heard a splat noise behind me, as something unspeakable hit the deck not far from my retreating feet. Worse yet, I could hear the rock apes running along the structure above me, attempting to keep pace as I ran for the nearest door.

The men showed not one jot of chivalry, all saving themselves with nary a thought for me as I ran with all my might to get inside. Running away from the apes as I was, I questioned if I should be throwing in a few zigzags to avoid their aim. Moving as fast as I could, I told myself they were monkeys, not the England cricket team. Surely, they couldn't hit a moving target.

With the final triumphant leap, I got inside the ship and the door slammed shut behind me, the men inside at least waiting for me there.

Half a dozen splat noises resounded as something hit the other side of the door. Now catching my breath, I questioned why the four gentlemen around me were all backing away.

I looked down at myself. There was a small brown mark just above my navel where the first piece of poop had landed, but only a nasty stain remained, the poop itself having dropped off in my flight.

Looking back up I asked, 'What?' I got no answer and their horrified faces caused me to look back down at my clothing. Now frowning with confusion, I asked again, 'What?'

Lieutenant Kashmir held up a hand, index finger extended downwards which he then rotated, silently suggesting that I should turn around to look at my back.

Not the most flexible person in the world, I twisted my shoulders one way and my head the other, to get a look at the back half of my body and that was when the foul stench hit me.

I was covered. There had to be thirty or maybe even forty splat marks, as the horrible, horrible apes had peppered me with poop.

Not willing to come any closer, Lieutenant Kashmir was nevertheless unbuttoning his white tunic.

'I think perhaps you might want to shed some of your clothing, Mrs Fisher,' he suggested. 'We can find a bag to put it in so it can be laundered.'

There was no hope I was ever putting any of these garments on again, no matter how clean they came out.

I wasn't exactly enthralled at the option of taking off my clothes. But I got the point that walking along the corridor on the upper deck of the ship wasn't a good idea either, and I certainly didn't want to take this poop back into my suite with me.

Gripping the bottom of my long-sleeved tee, I wished I'd put a camisole or something beneath it, instead of just my bra.

Seeing what I was about to do, four sets of male eyes widened with surprise, but not in a good way like my friend Barbie might get. It was not the excitement of seeing a naked woman I was witnessing on their faces, but the horror of an older woman taking off her clothing.

'Oh, um, there's a restroom just along the corridor,' Lieutenant Kashmir stuttered, wanting to stop me from stripping in public, but not wanting to get any closer to me.

To accentuate his desire to keep his distance, he held out his tunic, leaning forward from the waist to get as close to me as possible without moving his feet.

Grumpily, I snatched it from him and stomped down the corridor to find the ladies' restroom. Using the mirrors inside, I got to see the full horror that was Patricia Fisher covered in monkey poop.

My clothes got stuffed unceremoniously into the trash bin in the corner, I would advise someone it was there to come and deal with it later. My running shoes had poop on them too, so when I emerged from the restroom, wearing a smile, my underwear, and an oversized security officer's tunic, I was also barefoot.

The poop attack had strengthened my resolve at least. Though now, I was more inclined to go to the armoury, and have the crew dish out whatever weapons they fancied using to shoot a few Gibraltar Rock Apes. Dismissing the notion, though I admit it appealed, I led Sam and the other men to the nearest elevator.

It was time to get rid of our monkey problem.

Remarkable

My solution to the problem was a simple one. My question was all to do with what the apes were doing on the ship in the first place. What would drive a primate to leave its island home and come on board a cruise ship?

Obviously, I didn't really know the answer to that question, but I was willing to bet it was something to do with food and that was why I had almost two hundred crewmembers waiting for me outside storeroom four when I arrived.

On our way down through the ship, I collected the chief quartermaster, and the bursar. Those two men, whether they wanted to or not, were going to sign off on my plan. The quartermaster needed to account for what we were going to use, and the bursar needed to adjust the books accordingly, the pair of them ensuring that the ship was soon restocked.

They took in my outfit of choice, questions forming on their lips which they both chose not to pose when they saw the set of my mouth.

Finally arriving on deck six, I got the same looks and a susurration of whispered questions rippled through the crowd.

'The apes got my clothes!' I shouted to still the comments and remarks.

Most of the crew assembled and waiting for me had no idea what was inside storeroom four. This did not surprise me. The Aurelia is vast to say the least. Knowing what was behind every door and inside every storeroom would be like knowing what was behind every door in a city.

The only reason I knew was because a short while ago I had been involved in solving a mystery regarding somebody selling off supplies. As one might imagine, with thousands of passengers on board, and each of them eating a minimum of three meals a day, the Aurelia carried vast quantities of food.

We were going to use a small portion of it.

When I announced my plan, the bursar had asked, 'What do Gibraltar Rock Apes eat, Mrs Fisher?'

I gave him an honest reply, 'I have not the faintest idea. However, I'm sure if we lay them out an entire buffet of delights, and encourage them towards it, allowing them to pick their favourite nibbles will suffice.'

No one had a better idea, so Patricia Fisher's let's-feed-the-monkeys plan was the one we went with. Boxes and boxes of bananas, exotic fruits, nuts, breads, cakes, and other treats were taken from storeroom four, up and out through the crew exit, and onto the quayside where they were deposited in a pile fifty yards away from the ship.

As the mound grew - bemused passengers watching on as they queued to get back on board the ship - the rock apes began to appear. They were high above our heads, looking down through the railings.

Interrupting the trail of people traipsing across the quayside with more boxes, I decided the pile of food was high enough.

'Now let's leave a trail for them to follow,' I suggested. 'Who's got bananas?' I called. I didn't know whether monkeys actually ate bananas, or if that was just some wonderful cliché that everyone believed. Either way, I was going to find out. Employing half a dozen crew members to peel bananas, we opened two crates and started throwing the ripe fruit on the ground close to the ship, creating a line of them that led to the buffet feast.

‘All we need to do now, is back away, and wait for the magic to happen.’ I said this as confidently as I could, while also dismissing the crew members who had been helping me so that they could return to their normal tasks.

I kept a dozen volunteers with me, including Sam, plus Lieutenant Kashmir who wanted his tunic back, but also wanted to see if the crazy detective lady was actually as clever as she thought. He was not the only one to be open in his curiosity, as both passengers and crew began to line the decks in the places where the rock apes were not.

This included the captain, who was easy to pick out to my eye, and I got a small nod from him when he saw me looking in his direction. The nod could have meant anything, but I told myself he was congratulating me on a job well done.

Not that the stupid monkeys were taking the bait yet.

Just when I was beginning to think that I had wasted several thousand pounds worth of fresh fruit and other foods to achieve nothing, the apes began to leave the ship. Slowly at first, but then in a rush as those still on board watched the first ones begin to devour the abundance of food without them.

Standing barefoot on the Gibraltar quayside, with the crew preparing the ship to sail, I was surprised when I heard a person clapping.

One person quickly became two and then it seemed as if half the people on board were applauding me. Lieutenant Kashmir joined in, as did the other volunteers standing around me and Sam, of course.

Embarrassed by the praise I was receiving, I felt my face flush.

The issue with the primates was resolved, though I could not help thinking we needed a better solution for when the ship next came to Gibraltar. For now, though, the Aurelia appeared to be monkey free, but would they attempt to get back on board once they had finished the food?

I still had Lieutenant Kashmir's radio in my hand. I'd been using it to coordinate everyone for the last hour or so. Lifting it to my lips now, I pressed the send button, saying, 'Patricia Fisher for the captain.'

I was looking up at him high above my head on the top deck and waved my hand to make sure he was looking in my direction. I saw one of the officers standing next to him say something, Alistair's hand rising into sight to then be handed a radio.

'Congratulations, Patricia. That was quite remarkable,' he remarked.

'Thank you,' I accepted the compliment and moved quickly on. 'How soon before we cast off? I am concerned they might try to get back on the ship before we leave.'

'We shall be departing early for once,' he replied. Purple Star ships left on time, pretty much no matter what, so leaving early would raise a few eyebrows, but provided the passengers were back on board, I believed it wouldn't matter.

No sooner had he finished saying it than shore crew started to deal with the lines holding the ship in place.

Satisfied the task was complete and that I was no longer required, I said, 'I'm coming back on board now. Perhaps you can assign some crew to make sure the apes stay where they are,' I suggested.

'Of course,' he agreed. 'I do have one question though.'

'Yes?' I encouraged him to tell me what it was.

'Will you still be wearing just that tunic later?' I got to hear him chuckling just before he released the send button on his radio.

Treasure

Jermaine saw to it that Lieutenant Kashmir got his tunic back and I took another shower, convinced I must still smell of monkey poop despite being certain none of it had gone on my skin.

When I came back out into the main living area of my suite, Barbie was there.

'Hey, Patty,' she gave me an exuberant grin and a wave when she saw me. 'Whatcha been up to?'

My blonde Californian friend and roommate had been working in the gym all day and had a bowl of what appeared to be cold pasta in her hands now. She had probably consumed between four and five thousand calories already today and burned that off through continuous exercise. Nevertheless, dressed in skin-tight Lycra, she looked composed and as if she had just done her hair for the day. She sported a tan all year round, though I wasn't sure quite what her secret was, and rarely, if ever, wore any makeup. She just didn't need it.

She would be a very easy woman to hate, what with her natural blonde hair, gravity defying chest, and tiny waist, but I considered her to be a very good friend. She had put her life on the line to help me on more than one occasion - how does a person ever repay that?

I fired a smile in her direction in reply and took my eyes off her for a moment to nod my head towards Jermaine. He was in the kitchen area of my suite, looking at me expectantly. He did not need to voice the question he was asking, for we were both used to the routine of my life.

As he reached for the bottle of Hendricks gin chilling in the freezer, I turned my attention back to Barbie.

'I'm surprised you haven't heard how my day has been going,' I remarked. 'The body count since rising this morning stands at two, and I've trashed two outfits.' I left out the bit where the second one got covered in monkey poop, the poor girl was eating, and didn't need to hear about it.

Barbie snorted a laugh, unsurprised by the content of my report, but turned serious when she asked, 'Are we talking murders?'

I nodded in her direction, gratefully accepting the large balloon glass of gin and tonic from my butler as he crossed the room to hand it to me.

The dachshunds were eyeing me from the couch, sitting with their heads up, but not committed enough to get off the sofa yet. There was no sign of food for them, so their interest at this stage was minimal.

To answer her question, I said, 'One for sure, and one that I am really not sure about.'

'Jermaine said something about treasure,' Barbie mumbled between bites of pasta.

I swung my eyes in his direction, only to find his features emotionless. I narrowed my eyes at him slightly, and watched as his cheeks turned just a little bit red.

'You might want to come with me, actually,' I commented. 'It was your boyfriend who found the 'treasure',' I made quote symbols with both my hands when I said the word. 'And he's expecting me to visit the medical centre shortly to have a look.'

Barbie clearly didn't know all the details, because her eyebrows were rising now as she tried to decipher what I was saying.

I explained, 'Hideki found uncut gemstones inside the belly of the man we found murdered in the hold of the ship this morning. I have yet to work out who he is. Actually, I haven't put the slightest effort into finding out who he is yet, truth be told.' I admitted. 'I'm rather hoping that Baker and the rest of them might have got somewhere with it today. I need to check in with them as well,' I was making a mental list of things to do in my head.

Allowing myself a second to think, I lifted the freezing cold gin and tonic to my lips and took a hearty swig of the chilled liquid. It washed over my taste buds in a kaleidoscope of flavours, and my eyes closed as I savoured my favourite tipple.

When I opened my eyes again Barbie was staring at me with an amused expression.

Chewing on her bottom lip slightly as if trying to find the right words, Barbie said, 'I don't get quite the same thing from gin that you do. You drink it and you look like you're having a religious experience,' she observed.

Feeling my cheeks redden, I argued, 'No, I don't! Do I?'

I flicked my gaze between Barbie and Jermaine, neither one of them committing to a verbal response. Barbie forked the last morsel of pasta into her mouth and handed Jermaine her bowl and fork.

He took it with a slight incline of his head and retreated towards the kitchen as Barbie dabbed at her lips with a tissue.

'Are you going to see Hideki now then?' she asked. It was clear from her question that she intended to come along and that suited me just fine.

Sensing that I was about to go out, Anna and Georgie both bounced up and onto their paws.

'Not this time, girls,' I told them. 'Mummy is going to the medical centre. It's not really a place for dogs.'

Demonstrating that they had no idea what I was talking about, both dogs leapt off the sofa and ran to the door. Jermaine, dutiful as always, was on his way to collect them long before I needed to do anything.

With two miniature sausage dogs tucked under his left arm, my butler opened the main door to my suite with his right and stood back so that we could exit.

After thanking him and promising that we would be back for dinner, Barbie and I made our way along the passageway towards the elevator. On the way down to find her boyfriend, Barbie quizzed me about the day's events, and in particular, the mysterious man we had found deep in the hull of the ship.

Lieutenant Commander Baker, and Lieutenants Bhukari, Schneider, and Pippin all arrived less than a minute after Barbie and I walked through the doors of the medical centre. The ship has several first aid posts to deal with the thousands of passengers on board and had a well-equipped medical centre located among the passenger decks. However, below the lowest passenger deck in the crew area, one could find an operating theatre and a morgue, both of which were unfortunately necessary on occasion.

The team of four security officers, assigned to me specifically from ship's security joined us because I invited them to do so. Since leaving them to deal with the Turkish passport thieves this morning, they had been working on a number of things and it was time for us to have a proper catch up.

They were not yet aware of the surprising items found in the murdered man's gut, so that was what I led with upon their arrival.

Barbie and I were already looking at the kidney bowl containing the colourful gemstones.

'What have you got there, Mrs Fisher?' asked Lieutenant Commander Baker, leading his team through the door.

Barbie answered for me, 'Come and see,' she invited, the excitement she felt evident in her voice.

Hideki had, of course, been good enough to clean the items we were inspecting, so that when the four newcomers gathered around, what they could see looked like coloured pebbles.

Lieutenant Pippin asked, 'Okay, what are they?'

Hideki, who was sitting on a wheelchair a yard or so away as he typed notes on a computer, kicked off to whiz the chair across to us. Using a pen that he pulled from behind his right ear, he pointed at a red pebble.

'That's a ruby,' he stated. Moving his pen to the stone next to it, he said, 'I'm fairly certain that is a diamond. These two are emeralds, that's definitely another ruby.'

He was cut off from identifying any more of the coloured pebbles by Lieutenant Bhukari asking, 'Where did they come from?'

Hideki supplied the answer. 'They were in the stomach of the man found on deck three this morning. Given their position in his body, he must have ingested them within six hours of dying. Any longer and they would have begun to work their way farther through his alimentary canal.'

Speaking before anyone else had a chance to, I said, 'Suddenly, we have a motive for his murder. Now all we need to do is find out who he is, where on earth he got these gemstones, and then attempt to figure out who killed him. Did you get anywhere with identifying him today?' I asked.

My team of four all lifted their faces from the kidney bowl of uncut gemstones to look at me, and then at each other.

'Not so far,' admitted Lieutenant Commander Baker. 'You were right in your guess that he doesn't appear to be a passenger. There is no record of anyone going missing, and we have no cabins with single passengers unaccounted for. In essence, he probably was a stowaway.'

Lieutenant Schneider picked up one of the stones, a ruby, if Hideki was to be believed.

'A stowaway with a big secret,' he remarked. 'This is not your average mystery.' He bounced the ruby into the air from his hand, catching it again and then repeating the motion, an absent-minded action as he thought. 'This is a fairly big stone,' he pointed out.

I thought about the five-carat sapphire Alistair bought me earlier today. The ruby in Lieutenant Schneider's hand had to be four times as big. I knew it would reduce in size when cut, but that did not detract from the fact that it was quite a hunk of rock. Not only that, it wasn't the biggest on display.

We could get the stones valued at some point, potentially when we arrived at our next destination. However, unless Hideki was wrong, which I did not think he was, and these were worthless pieces of glass, which I was fairly certain they were not, then the man had deliberately ingested a fortune in gemstones.

Where had they come from? Who was he? And who had killed him? A different person, a person who wasn't me, might be wishing it was somebody else's problem to deal with. Not me though. Oh, no, I was positively giggling with glee at how easy this was all going to be.

If only someone would give me a difficult task.

Sighing internally, and pushing the challenging mystery to one side, I asked Dr Nakamura about Evelyn Goodwin.

'Well, she definitely died of a heart attack. I've been able to pinpoint the time of death to between 2300hrs last night and approximately midnight. I can also confirm she was engaged in sexual activity immediately prior to her death.'

'Was her heart in poor condition?' Barbie asked.

Hideki nodded. 'Yes, most of her arteries were blocked. A heart attack was inevitable at some point.'

I doubted that would be much comfort to her nearest and dearest, and though it would be nice to record that she died of natural causes, I still wasn't one hundred percent convinced.

'What else could it have been?' I pressed him to give it some more thought.

He blinked his eyes, frowning slightly. 'It was a heart attack.'

I grimaced. 'Yeah, I don't really get people dying of heart attacks. Patricia Fisher, ship's detective, that's the title of a person who tracks down crazed killers exacting revenge for imagined slights. I bet she was murdered.'

'No' Hideki shook his head. 'She died of a heart attack.'

'How about an undetectable poison?' I asked. 'Could someone have slipped a little something in her drink?'

Hideki eyed me suspiciously, trying to work out if I was being serious or not.

'I performed a toxin screen on her blood, Mrs Fisher. There was no poison in her body.'

'Well, you wouldn't find it if it is an undetectable poison, would you?' I felt I had to point out the obvious.

Hideki looked around the room, silently asking someone to help him out. When he got nothing, he said, 'I'm not sure such a thing exists, Mrs Fisher.'

'Ha! The perfect way to get away with murder then. We'll just leave that on the table for now, shall we?' Turning my attention back to the team, I asked, 'Did you get anywhere with the missing five hundred dollars?'

Lieutenant Bhukari had been heading that part up, while Baker and Schneider were dealing with the Turkish passport thieves. We all looked inward to see what she would have to say.

'Not so far,' she admitted, sounding somewhat embarrassed to reveal there was yet another case where we were making no progress. 'She withdrew the money from the ATM outside the casino bar on deck seventeen at 2042hrs. There were no other receipts in her purse to indicate she made any purchases, and there were no bags in her cabin to suggest she went shopping with the money.'

Baker said, 'There were no casinos open last night. So she couldn't have frittered it away worthlessly on a blackjack table.'

'No,' Deepa agreed. 'Currently I am at a loss to explain where the cash went. As I pointed out earlier, there was no indication that she had been robbed.'

I summarised what we knew in a few words, as much for my own brain as anyone else's.

'We have a lady who may have died of natural causes or,' I swung my eyes to look at Hideki, 'may have been murdered using a sophisticated undetectable poison which stopped her heart and made it look like a heart attack.'

Sotto voce Hideki muttered, 'It was a heart attack.'

Ignoring him, I carried on with what I was saying. 'She may or may not have been robbed, but was most definitely positioned when she died to make it appear as if she died in her sleep, and she was with a man immediately prior to her fatal heart attack.'

Lieutenant Commander Baker remarked, 'We need to find out who that man is. We cannot conscionably put this case to rest until we can be sure that no crime has been committed.'

No one argued, the entire team quite committed to doing precisely what he just said.

'Then we have a third case, yes?' I prompted the team to tell me all about Tim Oswald and the gold-digger targeting his rich father.

Our business in the medical centre was already concluded. For now, at least. Lieutenant Pippin took the gemstones into custody, signing the appropriate paperwork to maintain the chain of evidence. They would be locked away securely until such time as we had something to do with them.

We couldn't hold onto them, and they had to belong to someone, though I had to wonder just how long this mystery was going to take to solve.

Travelling back up through the ship, crammed inside an elevator, the six of us discussed Miss Betty Ross.

'She's got the goods for it,' Lieutenant Pippin remarked, his cheeks flushing immediately when Lieutenant Bhukari frowned at him.

Turning her attention away from him to look at me, she remarked, 'What Anders means is that she has a rather impressive chest and is happy to display ninety-five percent of it seemingly regardless of what outfit she is wearing.'

While Baker and Schneider exchanged a look with Pippin and he attempted but failed to surreptitiously gesticulate the enormity of Betty Ross's boobs, Deepa provided us with a more accurate description.

'She has a generous D cup, and she's a US size four,' she added in deference to UK sizes being different to how they measure things across the pond. 'I would say her blonde hair is not natural, but it's been well done, and she looks every bit the part of the bimbo. I should imagine she's turning a lot of men's heads. Quite why she picks a man in his eighties ...' she stopped herself and restarted. 'Well, I think we're all in agreement as to why she's picked a man in his eighties. Now all we've got to do is catch her with possessions she has stolen from the Oswalds or catch her in the act of stealing them.'

Without warning, Deepa's right elbow jabbed out and back, connecting with her husband's ribs as he shared a lecherous exchange with the other boys in the elevator.

With three cases to keep us busy, and finite resources, we all knew there was only so much we could do. Under the belief that the stowaway's killer was most likely not on board, and even if he was, would take the greatest amount of work to identify, I elected to pause that investigation. At least, for now. We would circle back to it when we had the opportunity.

To tackle the other cases, I split the team into two. I would be looking into both, supported by Sam, while Deepa and Pippin watched Priscilla Purcell – I was suspicious enough to have them tail her - Baker and Schneider were going to be looking into Tim Oswald's case. Did we have a gold-digger on board? It sure sounded like it and if she had stolen some things then I expected we would catch her, and it wouldn't take too much effort. The guys were just going to create a background picture for the case and leave it until the morning.

I was more interested in our mysterious posed body. My senses were telling me it was a murder. A murder so clever even the doctor performing the autopsy was fooled. I had no idea how, but I was prepared to break a few rules to find out. I wanted to have a look around Priscilla's cabin when she wasn't there and would be taking a peek inside her handbag too if I got the chance.

Tasks assigned, we split up. Everyone needed to eat, and though most of us would be working on at least one of the cases at some point this evening, my team had already put in a full day, and deserved to have some rest.

I was set to have dinner with Alistair, where unfortunately, we still needed to discuss those wretched complaints. It still shocked me that someone had chosen to besmirch my good name and though I was convinced it was deliberate on someone's part, because I knew what they were claiming could not be true, I could not come up with one person who might be to blame for it.

Had I known the truth, I might have jumped off the boat and swam back to Gibraltar.

Under Pressure

'You know this is a pack of lies, right?' I fixed Alistair with a look that challenged him to suggest the letters I was holding in my hands could be anything else.

He had given me printed copies of the emails Purple Star Lines HQ had received to make reading them together easier. They were all from different people, whose presence on board the ship had been confirmed, and cross referenced to be sure that they and I could have crossed paths. However, I had no knowledge of any of the incidents about which they had been so incensed they felt a need to write to the cruise line.

Alistair nodded apologetically. 'I felt quite sure that they were, darling. Unfortunately, Purple Star Lines received them first. People there are asking questions, as one might expect. I assured them, of course, that this had to be some kind of mistake, or perhaps as you have suggested, a personal attack. Unfortunately, they are demanding I get a grip on the situation, and either prove unequivocally that you are not guilty, or remove you from your post.'

My jaw dropped open. Remove me from my post? I'd only just started!

Heading me off before I could start talking, Alistair asked, 'Is there anyone you could think of who you have upset since you came on board? Someone who would want to damage your reputation?'

With my teeth clenched firmly together, I shuffled the loose-leaf pages of A4 back into a neat pile and tapped them on the table so they were neat. Then I read the name signed off at the bottom of the first email.

'Ian Rosewater. He's reported that I burst into his cabin looking for drugs. Clearly that didn't happen, so I think that we should find this gentleman and ask him why he reported that it did.' I was going to face my accusers and beat the truth out of them if I needed to.

Alistair made a kind of 'Oops' face.

'He is no longer on board, dear. He and his wife departed when we docked in Sicily,' Alistair let me know, his tone at least sad about the fact that my accuser had already escaped.

I crumpled that piece of paper and flung it over my shoulder while scanning to find the name at the bottom of the next email. Alistair interrupted me.

'I'm afraid I've already conducted this exercise, dear. None of the people on these emails are still on board. Several of them terminated their cruises early and cited their experience with you as the reason for cancelling the rest of their trip. Most promised they would never sail with Purple Star again.'

I threw my arms in the air unable to believe what I was hearing.

'Just tell me, Alistair, that you don't believe it, please. That has to be the minimum starting point for me.'

'Of course I don't believe it, Patricia. But surely you understand that it doesn't matter what I believe. It only matters what I can prove. At this point, I can't prove anything, and Purple Star are breathing down my neck.'

Genuinely, I felt like raging at him. He ought to have been the first to leap to my defence, telling the people at Purple Star that they were being conned. I had a belly filled with fire, but I could not allow myself to vent my frustration at poor, dear Alistair. He was, I could see, in a tricky position. The whole ship's detective thing was an experiment, and thus far it was failing.

I closed my eyes and took a very deep breath, drawing air into my lungs and holding it there for a moment as I centred my chi or some other such nonsense. Whatever it was I was doing, it was the equivalent of counting to ten while I forced myself to calm down.

Opening my eyes again and exhaling, I said, 'I will investigate this in the morning. It can just be added to my list of other tasks. Someone is out to get me, and I'm going to find out who it is. When I do ...' I let my sentence tail off, unsure quite how I wanted to finish it. Murdering the person or persons behind it held a degree of attractive allure, though obviously I wouldn't do that. I wasn't sure what I would do, the old line about first digging two graves when one sets out on revenge came to mind.

I would need to clear my name, that would have to be a priority, forcing the person behind these lies to admit the truth.

It was dinner time, Alistair and I having planned a quiet meal in his cabin. My appetite was gone though, and we were quiet throughout the meal. Mostly this was down to me, and my brain working ten to the dozen as I sifted through events that had taken place since I came on board the ship just a couple of weeks ago.

For the life of me I could not come up with one person who I had upset, apart from those who had wound up being taken into custody by my team. I did not think this was a petty criminal coming back at me though. Rather, I was telling myself it had to be someone from my past.

Unfortunately, that created a long list.

Just before nine o'clock, I declared my intention to return to my suite. I simply wasn't in the mood for anything else, and I think it came as no great surprise to Alistair who was mature enough to be able to sense my emotional state.

He kissed me lightly on the lips and tried to tell me not to worry. He was going to continue to represent me to Purple Star. In his words, it would take a direct order from them to change my position on the ship. He didn't comment upon how likely he thought that order might be, and I was wise enough to not ask.

On my way back to my cabin, Anna and Georgie leading the way as usual, I heard my phone beep from somewhere in the depths of my handbag. I wasn't carrying my radio because I was off duty for the evening, but equally, I wasn't expecting anyone to want to get hold of me either.

My screen displayed the start of a text message. It was from Lieutenant Pippin, the youngest member of my team. With a swipe of my finger, I opened the message fully so that I might read it. It became quickly obvious that young Anders Pippin had chosen to continue working the case in his own time.

I say 'the' case, but of course we had several currently ongoing. The one to which I am referring is the rather suspicious circumstances of Evelyn Goodwin's death.

In the message, Lieutenant Pippin outlined that he had been examining CCTV footage of the deceased and her sister, Priscilla, going to dinner at La Trattoria Italian restaurant last night. He had something to show me in the morning when I was up. Clearly, he had not expected me to read the message this evening.

'Mrs Fisher?' he said my name as if surprised that I was calling him when he answered the phone.

'Yes, Anders, I just received your message. I'm on my way back to my suite, do you have something interesting to show me?'

He made a hmmming noise to himself before answering. 'I think so,' he replied, sounding a little uncertain. 'At least, what I mean is, I thought I did. There's a chap who meets the sisters when they leave the restaurant. I've been able to identify who he is from the ship's central registry.' He referred of course to the onboard computer system that registered everybody's face, passport details, and other important information, 'but I don't think he can be the one who was with Mrs Goodwin last night,' Anders concluded.

I had come to a halt in the passageway, pausing my forward motion because I wasn't sure which direction I wanted to go. The dachshunds were looking up at me, questioning looks on their faces as they wondered where it was we were supposed to be going. To aid me in reaching a decision, I questioned what Lieutenant Pippin was trying to tell me.

'Why couldn't he be the one?'

I got the same hmming noise again; Pippin trying to work out what he wanted to say.

'Well, he's travelling with another man. They're staying in a cabin on deck nine. Also, they have the same last name, so my assumption, which I accept could be wrong, is that they are a gay couple. I feel a little silly now, truth be told. I should have checked a little further before I sent you that message. I thought I was onto something for a moment.'

'No apology required, Anders. We often have to follow up a number of leads before we find one that proves helpful.' His suggestion that a gay man travelling with his husband was unlikely to have engaged in bedroom activities with a lady seemed valid. However, I had too much going on in my brain to consider getting to bed yet, so I asked Lieutenant Pippin where he was.

Getting my answer, I gave the dog lead a little tug to get the girls moving and set off to find him.

False Lead

The ship's security team have operation rooms on every deck. They have a number of functions to perform on board, though for the most part the passengers just see them as another of member of crew. They are used to it and have been trained to respond generously when passengers pose questions about arrival times at the next port or what time the ice cream parlour on deck seventeen opens. When on duty, they are expected to patrol the ship, making sure to be on hand should any situation arise that might require their assistance. Of course, they cannot patrol all the time, so they retire to operations rooms to cool off, remove their hats, and relax for a while.

My team had been afforded their own operations room. It was on deck ten, a repurposed meeting room that we could use to record information and meet up to discuss ongoing cases. The walls were adorned with whiteboards, and in the centre was a quad of desks with four computers and a projector aimed at one wall.

I found Lieutenant Pippin alone in our operations room.

'This is very diligent of you, Anders,' I remarked, breezing through the door with the dachshunds racing ahead. They knew a sucker when they saw one and Anders was already bending down to greet them, happy to hand out ear scratches and belly rubs to my pair of dopey sausage dogs.

Combining the task of petting my dogs with responding to my comment, Anders nodded his head towards the screen on his desk.

'I've got it right here if you'd like to see it, Mrs Fisher.'

I walked around the room, coming up behind Pippin where he sat behind a keyboard facing the door. The footage was frozen, the rather blurry image easily identifiable as the tables and chairs arranged outside La Trattoria.

Abandoning the task of scratching my dogs, Pippin tapped the mouse button, and the video feed began to roll.

'That's Mrs Goodwin and her sister right there,' Anders used the nib of a pencil to indicate where I needed to look. 'They have just paid the waiter and are about to leave.'

I watched in silence for twenty seconds, waiting for something to happen. The ladies remained in their seats, talking about something. The camera had to be mounted high above the restaurant on the edge of the opening that plunged through the decks in the middle of the ship. Letting in sunlight and creating the feeling of space, the opening sat in the centre of the ship where most of the restaurants and shops are located.

The shot we had was from too far away to make out much detail but when the ladies stood to leave the restaurant, I could tell it was Evelyn and Priscilla – two sisters on their way to the Caribbean.

Just as Lieutenant Pippin had claimed, a man approached them as they were leaving the restaurant. I hadn't noticed him until that point, but he had been standing just a few yards away from the entrance, clearly waiting for them to make their way into the open.

He was handsomely dressed in a nice suit, his dark brown hair shot through with a little grey around the sides. I couldn't see his face, but to dispel any suggestion that he might have been asking them the time or something equally innocuous, both ladies linked their arms with his and the three of them strolled away from the camera like Dorothy and friends on the yellow brick road.

'That's all we've got from that camera,' Pippin remarked, fiddling with the mouse again to open a different tab on the bottom of his screen. 'We don't see his face at all there and it took me a little while to find it.'

Guessing, I asked, 'Does he appear when Evelyn is withdrawing her cash?'

I got a quick shake of Pippin's head in response. 'No, that's what I expected. But he doesn't come into the frame of the camera above the ATM at any point. I think all we see are his shoes. That's a little tenuous, I realise but I think they are the same shoes, which places him at the ATM with her. Anyway, to identify him, it took me a while to find a camera where it captures his face.'

I could not guess how long the young security officer had been at the task, but it must have been some hours because he had randomly found the man walking past the camera mounted above the door to a cabaret bar on deck eighteen.

There was little doubt in my mind that we were looking at the same man. The suit and hair and the shape of his body were all precisely the same.

As he explained on the phone, Lieutenant Pippin then went on to establish who it was that we were looking at. The man in question was an Italian by the name of Ricardo Rossini. He was travelling with his husband, Claude Rossini. They were both quite handsome and in their fifties.

Anders gave me enough time to absorb the information before asking me, 'So what do you think, Mrs Fisher?'

I sucked a little air through my teeth and gave him a shrug.

‘I think it's really solid detective work, but I also think you're right, and this is a dead end. Perhaps tomorrow we should follow up and ask Mr Rossini the nature of his relationship with Mrs Goodwin and her sister. Clearly he knew them, but he may not know that Evelyn passed away last night. We can ask him a few questions and see whether we think he's answering truthfully or not.’

With something akin to a motherly instruction to give up for the night and go to bed, I collected my dogs, and proceeded to do precisely that myself.

Giving me the Willies

The morning sun shone behind the curtains in my bedroom, filling the room with a softly filtered version of the bright light outside. It was still early, the giant ball of fire barely above the horizon, but it was already time for me to be out of my bed.

Many months ago when I first came on board, I committed to losing a few pounds and getting fit. At the time, the desire to change my body shape had been almost all about catching my husband with another woman and unhealthily choosing to blame myself.

Once I got my head straight again, I decided to keep on with the exercise regime because it was making me feel more in control of my life. I lost weight as a result, not as an aim, and have kept it off. I have a new man in my life now and though I wouldn't say that I was staying the shape I am for him – perish the thought – I am conscious of my figure.

With that in mind, and because I have a physical trainer as my live-in cabin-mate, I was going for a run.

Before I left the operations room last night, I remembered to collect a new radio. It was good practice to keep them with us at all times, but I didn't think that needed to extend to when I was going for a run.

Anna and Georgie eyed me suspiciously from their bed in the corner of my room while I pulled on my gym gear and a new pair of running shoes. On occasion, I made them come with me. They did not approve of running unless there was something to chase, but I only took them when it was just me and I could get away with going slow. That was not going to be the case today.

Barbie was in the suite's main living area waiting for me. At least, I had to assume it was Barbie for what I could see was a young women's derriere and legs. As if chopped off at the waist, the top half was missing.

Barbie – it was her, obviously – was bent at the waist to place her forehead against her shins – part of her stretching routine. If I attempted to achieve the same manoeuvre, my spine would ping off across the room like a broken spring.

Hearing me come in behind her, she unfolded to her full, almost six-foot, height and said, 'Come on, let's go.'

Her normal smile was missing, making me wonder if there had been a disagreement between her and Hideki. I elected to wait and see if she brought the subject up, vowing to ask her if everything was okay in a little while if she didn't.

A minute later, I realised my error, when the deficit of oxygen in my lungs, and consequently the rest of my body, demanded I focus on breathing and forget even attempting to speak until much, much later.

We kept going like that, Barbie pushing the pace far harder than normal until I started to fall behind. Then she started shouting at me to, 'Keep going,' and to, 'Push harder.'

I did precisely that, forcing my body to the point of discomfort and beyond. My legs began to protest, the muscles feeling heavy as my lungs failed to keep up with their demands for oxygen.

When sparkly lights began to appear in front of my eyes, I ignored Barbie's encouragement – not that she sounded all that motivational today, mostly she sounded angry – and slowed my pace until I was almost walking.

I had a stitch in my side, and couldn't speak, such was the heaving nature of my breathing as I fought to get air in.

Barbie slowed too, but only so she could shoot me a disgruntled frown. Without another word, she twisted to face the way we had been going and left me where I was. All I could do was stare at her back as it vanished along the deck and out of sight.

Whatever was bothering Barbie, it had to be something bad. She was always so positive about everything; she was a breath of fresh air everywhere she went. She had certainly never once shown me a negative emotion and yet today she had run off and left me gasping for breath as if I was somehow behind whatever was bothering her.

I walked, my hands behind my head, until I got my breath back enough to start jogging again. Hoping that I might run into Barbie and expecting that she would be embarrassed by her actions and want to talk about what was bothering her, I kept going. However, I completed my usual route around the open upper deck of the ship twice and failed to spot her at any point.

Arriving back at my suite, I was surprised to find that I had missed Barbie. According to Jermaine, she called out that she needed to get to work, went into her room to shower and change, and left the suite a few minutes later. He had coffee waiting for me and was in the kitchen ready to prepare whatever it was that I desired for breakfast.

'Jermaine, dear, something is bothering Barbie. Has she said anything to you?' I inquired. Jermaine and Barbie had come onto the ship together and had been very good friends ever since. They spent a lot of their free time together, though less so now that Barbie's boyfriend was on the ship.

Jermaine handed over a steaming mug of coffee and turned back toward the kitchen when he replied.

'I couldn't possibly say, madam.'

I warmed my hands on either side of the coffee cup, pondering whether I should go and find her in the upper deck executive gymnasium where she worked, or leave her to work things out for herself. She knew that I was there for her if she ever needed anything, I was confident of that. And she knew that she could come to me about anything. Acknowledging that she wasn't a little girl and would involve me when she felt it was appropriate, I elected to give her the space she needed.

Sipping at my coffee, I said, 'Well, something is troubling her. I hope she shares it with us soon. If you get the chance, you may want to politely enquire.'

I felt like eating carbs this morning, I had certainly burnt off a good few calories already, so I left Jermaine poaching some eggs that he would serve me on some wholemeal bread, with a side of spinach and some slices of ham. That would be quite sufficient to carry me through to the middle of the day.

Picking up my radio when I got out of the shower, I pressed the send button and called for Lieutenant Commander Baker.

He responded almost immediately. 'We are currently en route to the Platinum Suite, Mrs Fisher. Actually, we just arrived. There has been a development. Are you able to join us?' I could hear Lieutenant Schneider speaking in the background, his Austrian accent easy to pick out.

'Do I have time for breakfast?' I asked.

Something smashed loudly at the other end, and I grumpily accepted that breakfast was going to have to wait.

I told Baker I would be right there, put the radio down and cracked my door to yell to Jermaine that his breakfast efforts were for naught.

'I shall make you one of Miss Berkeley's power shakes, madam,' his voice carried through the closing bedroom door as I hurried to find clothes and get dressed.

Two minutes later, with my butler scurrying along behind me, my dachshunds leading the way as they charged to get to wherever we were going, and fumbling fingers trying to tuck my blouse into the waistband of my trousers, I more or less ran to the other side of the ship to find the current residents of the Platinum Suite.

I could hear the shouting thirty seconds before I found its source. The door was ajar, a thin crack of daylight showing through from the other side. Lieutenant Pippin was on the other side, minding the suite's exit while Baker, Schneider, and Bhukari attempted to cool things down.

Their butler, all part of the top suite's package, was standing to one side. I knew his name – Bartholomew, but wasn't sure we had ever spoken.

'She is a thief, Dad!' shouted a man I immediately guessed was Tim Oswald, the one who filed the complaint and asked us to prove Betty Ross was guilty. His accent was midwestern US somewhere or possibly New England – I never had been very good with American accents.

Betty Ross was just as easy to pick out, and not just because she swore at Tim and denied his accusation. She was tall at close to six feet, blonde just as Deepa described her, and sported a tiny waist and impressive chest which jiggled and heaved as she ranted. She looked a bit like a blonde

Betty Boop doll. She was English – something I hadn't expected, her accent pure Newcastle and I wondered if anyone else in the room could understand her when she spoke fast.

'The only thing I have stolen is your father's heart!' she shouted across the room. She was standing beside a man in his eighties, his hands on her shoulders as if there to keep her from running across the room to strike her accuser. 'And he stole mine!' she added, a tear slipping from her right eye to run down her cheek.

'You've no evidence, Tim!' complained the old man. I did not know the Oswalds or where they had amassed their fortune. Nor could I tell if their relationships were strained before Betty came onto the scene, but they were at each other's throats now.

'I demand you search her,' raged Tim, his words aimed at Lieutenant Commander Baker and his team. 'She has taken cash and items of jewellery from my room, and stolen from my daughter too.'

Betty thrashed to get away from her lover, successfully escaping his grip to then run at Tim.

Schneider stepped into her path, his hands out to stop her.

'Please, Miss,' he begged politely.

Betty screeched her outrage and frustration.

'It would appear,' I spoke for the first time, my voice drawing everyone's attention in my direction, 'that we can clear this up quite easily.'

'Who are you?' Tim Oswald wanted to know.

Lieutenant Commander Baker was good enough to name me.

'Sir, this is Patricia Fisher, the ship's detective. You may have heard of her.'

He frowned. 'No. Should I have?'

I focused my attention on the young woman in the middle of the argument.

'I am not emptying my handbag,' Betty snapped the moment she met my eyes.

Tim Oswald grasped her response and twisted it. 'Because it's full of jewellery stolen from us.'

Betty swung around, shoving into Lieutenant Schneider as anger stole her reason and she tried to go through him to get to Tim. All she succeeded in doing was squashing her ample chest up against the tall Austrian.

With another grunt of rage, Betty took a step back. 'Fine. You want to see what I have in my handbag. Go ahead.'

With that, she upended the Louis Vuitton bag which I guessed was probably a gift from Mr Oswald Senior – it probably cost more than her cruise. Tumbling to the carpet came lipstick, tissues, a tiny pair of lace knickers, a phone in a sparkly case, condoms, and other assorted paraphernalia, but no jewellery.

'Then you didn't put it in your handbag,' sneered Tim. 'She's probably got it hidden on her somewhere.'

'Oh, let it go, Dad,' sighed a new voice as a teenage girl of sixteen or maybe seventeen sloped into the suite's main living area. She had that sullen, bored tone all kids seem to perfect as they get toward the middle of their teens. Her hair was dyed black and dark red, her lips and nails were black to match, and her clothing, which looked to have lost a fight with a lawn mower, was also black where it wasn't shredded. There was a lip ring through her upper lip and piercings in her nose and right eyebrow.

'No!' he snapped, raising his voice to match his anger. 'She's not going to get away with it!'

Betty was lifting her top. She had on a miniskirt – with nothing under it I guessed from the pair of knickers now on the deck among the other items from her handbag – a pair of heels and a figure-hugging satin top. There was no bra beneath it, but just when I thought she was going to follow up the handbag trick by ripping off her clothes, she stopped.

'Where is it I am supposed to have hidden anything, Tim?' she demanded to know.

He met her gaze without flinching or changing his tune.

'I think we all know where you have put it.'

I didn't. At least not until Tim's daughter screwed her face up and said, 'Ewww. Well, if that's the case, she can definitely keep them.'

'You can search her,' Tim nodded his head at Lieutenant Bhukari.

Betty's eyes widened in shock.

'No one is searching anywhere!' she shrieked.

'Quite so,' I agreed.

Betty dropped the hem of her top and crouched to begin putting her things back into her handbag.

'Useless. You lot are absolutely useless,' Tim turned his ire against the security team. 'I am being systematically robbed and the thief is right there in front of you, yet you won't do a thing about it. Who is it that I send my complaints to?' he enquired, smiling at me pleasantly because he was cruel and petty.

Another complaint? What was it with everyone and their need to complain about me?

Betty placed the final item into her bag and stood up. Twisting on her heels to face Mr Oswald Senior, she said, 'John, I am leaving. I'm not coming back until you move to a new cabin or get rid of Tim.'

'I'm his son and heir!' Tim raged. 'Not some gold-digging harlot! Come to your senses, Dad,' he implored, switching from insulting Betty to begging his father. 'She is conning you, Dad. Don't you see that?'

'Because I am too old to be loved?' Tim's father challenged his son.

Tim's teenage daughter nodded her head vigorously, and said, 'And then some, Grandpa.'

John Oswald ignored his granddaughter, his focus never wavering from his son as he waited for an answer.

Tim hung his head.

'No, Dad. You know that's not what I am saying, but you are eighty-two, Dad and ... Betty,' he had to force himself to say the woman's name, 'is almost the same age as Tulisa.' He wafted one arm in his daughter's direction, making it clear he was referring to her.

'That shouldn't matter,' sobbed Betty. 'I'm not after his money. I'll sign paperwork if you want me to.'

Tim snorted derisively. 'How much was that handbag? Or those shoes?' he asked. 'How much was dinner last night? Caviar, champagne, and lobster, wasn't it?'

Betty looked at John, her bottom lip quivering.

'You don't think I'm with you for the money, do you, John?'

'Of course not,' John snapped, reacting as if her prompt had helped him to reach a tough decision. 'I need you to find somewhere else to stay, Tim.' He saw his son about to start protesting and raised a hand to stop him. 'At least until you can come to terms with our relationship. I want you out of this suite. I'm sure these fine people will assist you to find an empty cabin somewhere.'

Tim trembled he was so furious. He was losing and he didn't look like a man who was used to coming out anywhere but on top.

He shot a hate-filled grimace at Betty, raising a finger to point. 'I'm going to catch you. You see if I don't.' He shifted his eyes to glare at his father. 'I'll be ready to accept your apology when they place her in cuffs.'

His final words delivered, Tim stormed out of the living area and into a bedroom, the door slamming hard behind him.

In a quiet voice, Betty said, 'I'm going to go, John. Let me know when it is safe to return, please.'

They kissed, lip to lip like lovers though it wasn't a passionate embrace. When they parted, Betty made her way to the door, her head and eyes down so she wouldn't have to look at any of us as she left the suite.

I backed out of the door before she got there – I wasn't done with her yet.

Betty Ross

I sold Betty the idea of going through the metal detector device at the ship's entrance, telling her it would prove she wasn't lying about the jewels. She almost resisted, at which point I was going to have to insist, but thankfully, an escort in the form of Baker and his team wasn't necessary.

I borrowed Lieutenant Pippin to come with us, claiming I didn't know how to operate the device, which was true, but it wasn't the real reason for having him along. I didn't want to believe she had the missing jewellery, but if she did and she believed I was about to catch her with it, I couldn't guess how she might react.

Also, and rather obviously, if she did have the stolen goods hidden … ahem, about her person, then I needed Pippin on hand to arrest her.

Making our way down through the ship from the top deck, where we started, to deck seven where the metal detection equipment was situated, I engaged Betty in conversation, doing my best to make me seem like an ally or a friend in whom she could confide.

'How did the two of you meet?' I asked as an opener.

She didn't answer my question though, she answered the one she thought I was asking.

'You think it's weird, don't you?' she replied, quickly followed by, 'My friends do. I can't really explain it,' she mumbled, sounding embarrassed as she confided in me. 'I've never dated a guy who was more than a couple of years older than me until now. John … John has some kind of hold over me. He's just so … hot.' The word she finished the sentence with was the last one I could have ever imagined her using.

'Where are you sailing to?' I asked. I already knew her passage was due to have ended already.

'That's a little up in the air,' she replied with a shrug that made her look sad. 'John asked me to stay on board when the rest of my friends got off. He has a place in Connecticut – I had to look up where that is,' she admitted with a self-deprecating grin. 'I'm not sure what to do. He wants me to travel with him … to go home with him to Connecticut. I will have to quit my job and I won't get to see my mum.'

'What job do you have?' I asked.

'Oh, I'm a hairdresser,' she replied without needing to think. 'I always wanted to work in the beauty industry, and I landed a job with a top salon,' she boasted proudly.

I listened as Betty jabbered, her words falling in a nervous torrent. I would steer her to give me the information I wanted, if necessary, but all the while she wanted to talk, I was going to let her fill the world with words.

Mostly, Betty lamented meeting John. I suspected it to be an act, the young gold-digger looking for sympathy because she could not help how she felt about the geriatric billionaire. It was convincing though, her expression pained at times as she fought with what she claimed were conflicting emotions.

By the time the elevator carried us down to deck seven, I knew almost as much about Betty Ross as I did Barbie or Jermaine – the girl could talk. I knew long before we put her through the metal detector at the ship's entrance that it would return a nil result because the idea of going through it hadn't bothered her in the slightest.

'Is that it now?' she asked, timidly. 'Can I go?'

I nodded my head and smiled. 'Yes, Betty. Please enjoy the rest of your time on board the Aurelia,' I employed a line I heard Alistair use often, 'and thank you for helping us with our enquiries.'

Lieutenant Pippin escorted her to the elevator and made sure she was set to get back to her cabin. When the doors swished shut and the car was moving, he turned to me.

'She was lying, right?' he asked.

'About which bit? Her feelings for a man old enough to be her grandfather? Or the bit about not stealing anything from the billionaires?'

Pippin gave me an uncertain look. 'Um, yes? Both, either? What do you think, Mrs Fisher?'

'I think we need to track her movements. She didn't have the jewellery on her, but that doesn't mean she hasn't stashed it in the Platinum Suite for later retrieval. I'm willing to believe it is missing and since we are talking about multiple items, I think we can assume it has been stolen.'

Pippin caught onto what I was saying.

'So, we are dealing with a cool customer. You think maybe she is a pro criminal?' I knew he was asking because we met two such ladies a short while ago. Mavis and Agnes, a pair of ageing, Irish con artists and thieves, had been using their looks to rip men off for decades. Part of me knew they ought to be behind bars, but acknowledging that they had come to my rescue more than once and had (more or less) given up their criminal ways to settle down with two of my friends, I had to accept that not all criminals go to jail.

Besides, that pair would just let themselves out again if they were ever locked up.

To answer the young lieutenant, I said, 'That's for us to find out. Someone has stolen from one of the Aurelia's top paying passengers and Purple Star is going to hear about it if we fail to catch the person behind it.'

We had waited for the elevator car to return and were still chatting as it began ascending through the ship once more.

'So what's our next step?' Pippin asked me.

I had multiple cases to investigate, and I was finding it tough to prioritise.

'I am going to find Mr Oswald. The junior Mr Oswald that is. I need a complete description of the missing jewellery.'

'Oh, we already have that, Mrs Fisher,' Pippin pointed out. Of course they did, my team were furiously efficient.

'Nevertheless,' I replied. 'I think I would benefit from some time spent calmly discussing the circumstances of his father's relationship with Miss Ross.' I didn't know what I would gain from it – in truth I don't really know how it is that I come to work out the solution to most of the cases I investigate. The answers just sort of come to me if I expose myself to enough information. 'He will be moving to a new suite, I assume. Can you find out which one it is, please?'

Lieutenant Pippin was on his radio a second later, talking to his actual boss, Lieutenant Commander Baker.

Placing one hand over his radio mouthpiece – a redundant action since all he needed to do was not press the send switch – he relayed the information Baker had just given him.

'Deck 19, suite thirty-two.'

The suites on deck nineteen were among the ship's most popular and as expensive as even high-earning passengers could afford. Only the superrich and middle-aged women with Maharajas behind them could afford such luxury as one found on the top deck. However, the suite he was now in might be palatial to most people on board, but I expected to find Tim Oswald was unhappy about it and I was not to be disappointed.

Buddy

Before I got to Mr Oswald Junior, I chose to familiarise myself with the Oswald family members, Miss Ross and her friends. They would all be logged in the ship's central registry system, even the friends of Miss Ross who had already left the ship. It was a task I could delegate and then have someone give me the highlights, but I knew the team was working to determine the identity of the murdered stowaway and piecing together the last movements of Mrs Evelyn Goodwin and her sister. That would keep them busy and there was no need to trouble them with trivia I could investigate for myself.

The dachshunds barked as I swiped my key card and came into the suite, Jermaine appearing as if by magic to take my bag and coat before the door even closed.

Arriving half a second later, Anna and Georgie ran straight up my legs looking for pick ups and kisses.

'Something to refresh you, madam?' offered Jermaine as I carried both tiny dogs back into the living area.

'A coffee?'

Jermaine nodded curtly, hung my jacket on a hanger to ensure it kept its shape and crossed the suite at a sedate butler's pace to the kitchen where I soon heard him pouring water into the coffee machine.

I got as far as the desk, a large mahogany thing with four thick carved legs and a leather thing inset into the top. I believed the leather was to make writing by hand more comfortable but that was wasted on me.

Settling into the ridiculously comfortable leather chair – honestly, it felt like it had been carved out of clouds – I settled the dogs on my lap. From underneath the desktop, I slipped out a small shelf on which a keyboard and mouse were hidden. With a wiggle of the mouse, a large monitor at the back of the desk came to life.

Having access to the ship's central registry and thus the ability to interrogate it for passenger and crew information was a new thing. Previously, I had depended upon Jermaine and Barbie to do such things for me, but now I had a higher clearance level than most crew members.

Finding the details I wanted took only seconds – the system was highly user-friendly. I checked out Betty first, looking at what information we had recorded and at her friends. Betty's passport picture showed her natural dark brunette hair colour. Doing a little mental arithmetic, I figured out that the document had been issued when she was seventeen so the blonde hair could be a new thing or might be years old.

I could see nothing in anyone's file that triggered me to believe there was any reason to look further or deeper. It was the same with the Oswalds. I noted that Tulisa was older than I had previous believed. I had pegged her age at seventeen or possibly younger, but she was nineteen. I had to question what she thought about Betty's supposed infatuation with her grandfather.

In her passport picture, which was less than six months old, her lip ring and eyebrow piercing were missing, the small puncture wounds they left behind visible in the photograph. A bit like tattoos, the desire to put permanent holes in your face was a thing I didn't really understand. She would have to either have the embellishments in her face, or put up with the scars for the rest of her life.

Deciding there was nothing much to learn from looking at Tim Oswald's daughter, I switched back to Betty. On a whim, I looked up her next of kin contact details, finding a Mrs Helen Ross listed. I guessed it was her mother but would find out soon enough because I was calling the number.

It connected instantly, rang twice, and was answered by a woman with a voice so gravelly she had to smoke two packs a day.

'Who's this?' she barked into my ear. 'Is this telemarketing? Because if you are going to try to sell me something, I can assure you I'm not buying. I haven't got enough money to keep the electric running.' Apparently, that was funny to Helen Ross who proceeded to cackle down the phone line and then start coughing. It was the type of cough one hears from a long-time smoker – that deep, rattly bark that goes on and on until the person finally wrestles it under control.

'Mrs Ross, I have no intention of selling you anything,' I advised once I believed she could hear me. 'My name is Patricia Fisher. I am the detective onboard the Aurelia, the cruise ship on which your daughter, Elizabeth is sailing.'

I heard a tut and a sigh. 'Go on then. What's she done this time?' Betty's mother encouraged me to reveal. 'Has she been stealing?'

My eyes flared and I sat up straight in my chair, reaching into my handbag for a pen.

'Mrs Ross, does Elizabeth have a criminal record?'

'Elizabeth? You're just trying to confuse me. Her name is Betty,' Helen Ross insisted. 'No one's called her Elizabeth since her gran passed, God rest her soul. Has she got a criminal record? No. But that's only because she sweet talks the police every time they pick her up. She got fired from that nice hairdressing job for getting light-fingered with the takings. She said she needed money for the cruise she was going on with her mates.'

I got to hear Mrs Ross light a cigarette and take a deep pull on it. Like her daughter, she liked to talk. She jabbered on for a bit but told me nothing new. I had enough though. I was suspicious before and now I knew she had a history of thievery and using her looks to get her way. A chance to up her game came along, and she was looking at a big score from the Oswalds. Now I just had to catch her.

When I was finally able to get a word in, I ended the conversation and pushed back in the chair to let my mind simmer for a few seconds. Jermaine had been patiently waiting for my conversation to end and was standing, just out of sight, to my right. When I became aware of his presence there, I swivelled to face him.

'Your coffee, madam,' he announced lowering the silver tray so that I could take my cup.

I thanked him with a smile, lifting the cup and savouring the aroma as I brought it closer to my mouth. Then I threw the whole cup into the air, narrowly avoiding scalding my face as the steaming hot liquid flew by my left cheek.

It wasn't exactly a voluntary reaction, of course. The coffee launching came about due to the dachshunds choosing to explode. From my lap where they were already snoozing, heads on my right thigh, bottoms on my left, both dogs took off, using my lap as a launch pad as they dove into the air three feet off the carpet.

Hitting the deck, their paws already running, they shot across the room.

I was about to ask what on earth had gotten into them when I saw precisely what had driven them from their contented slumber.

There was a monkey on my sun terrace.

'Jermaine! There's a monkey on my sun terrace!' I blurted unnecessarily.

The doors were shut – they are kept that way when we are at sea to stop the breeze that blows through the suite, and it was a good thing too because Anna and Georgie were trying to eat their way through the glass.

'I believe that is a Gibraltar Rock Ape, madam.' Jermaine caught my expression, hastily adding, 'Not that the species is germane to the situation.'

'I thought we got them all,' I sighed.

The ape was sitting on the small dining table where I ate my meals on occasion.

'I'm going to have to get someone up here to help catch it. It can be secured in the hold and returned to Gibraltar later.'

There was no way the ape could have heard me, but he jerked his head in my direction at that precise moment, flipped me the finger, and vanished over the side of the ship.

I gasped in astonishment, instantly worried the poor animal had just fallen into the ocean. Jermaine got to the door before me, rushing for once so that I wouldn't have to open the doors myself.

The dogs spilled through the gap, their little tails wagging so hard they were like looking at hummingbird wings. The ape was gone, but his scent remained, and it was driving the dogs nuts.

At the edge of the ship, I leaned over and scanned the water, my eyes drawn instead to a flash of something brown and furry as it vanished into another cabin two decks below.

'Buddy is going to cause me a whole pile of grief, I can just see it,' I muttered.

Jermaine frowned in his lack of understanding.

'Buddy?'

'The monkey,' I explained. 'Ape rather,' I corrected myself. 'I just named him.'

'Do you think, madam, that there might be more than one who remained on board?' Jermaine asked.

I groaned. 'I certainly hope not. One is going to be hard enough to catch. I'll need to alert the crew.'

I retrieved my radio from my handbag, contacting the bridge where I left the displeasing news to be passed on to the deputy captain. There being little else I could do about it – it's not as if I could search the ship to find Buddy all by myself – I put the matter to one side and hoped I would find Tim Oswald in a better mood than he had been when we first met.

'Shall I make you another coffee, madam?' Jermaine enquired.

I shook my head. 'No, thank you. I shall be back for lunch I expect.' Using the toe of my shoes to nudge the girls back into the suite, I said, 'Come along, you two. You can be the calming influence. We'll get Sam too.'

Tim's Opinion

Tim Oswald might have been pleased to see me, but the message failed to ever reach his facial muscles.

'Can I come in, Mr Oswald?' I enquired politely, hovering in the passageway outside his suite. 'This is my assistant, Ensign Sam Chalk.' I indicated Sam who gave Mr Oswald a beaming grin.

He backed away from the door, muttering, 'If you think you can squeeze into this excuse for a cabin.'

I felt a desire to show him the cabins on deck seven where one really could not swing a cat. The people staying in them were having the time of their lives, enjoying a cruise they probably had to save for and thus appreciating all they had.

Had Tim been born into wealth? I didn't know whether his father had made the family fortune or if it might have been a great great-grandfather way back in the past. It made little difference, I decided because either way he was spoiled by what he had grown accustomed to.

Thankfully, once he closed the door, he softened a little.

'I had a dachshund when I was a boy,' he revealed, watching my girls snuffling the carpet near my feet. 'I wanted to get another when Tulisa was a little girl, but she was never interested in having a little dog. She wanted ponies,' he muttered, making it sound like a complaint.

'Do you mind if I let them off the lead?' I enquired, picking up on his interest in them.

He wafted a hand in my direction. 'By all means.'

The girls danced across the room the moment they were set free, snapping at each other in their excitement. Mr Oswald watched them until I spoke again.

'I need to ask you more about your father's relationship with Miss Ross, Mr Oswald. I assume you already know she was not carrying the missing jewellery earlier.'

I got a tight-lipped smile in return. 'So your team informed me. She took them though, and the thievery has been going on since my father first let her into the suite. I can handle my father making a fool of himself with a younger woman ... I applaud him almost. Goodness knows at his age there won't be many more chances to have that kind of fun, and it doesn't really bother me that he has been spending money on her – outfits and such. It's small change, but for her to then steal from us ... that's too much.'

'If she is guilty, I will catch her,' I claimed in a confident voice. I could have told him what I had learned from Betty's mother, but he would then confront her, or tell his father, and once she knew we were on to her, she would ditch all the evidence, wherever it might be hiding, and make it far harder for us to catch her. So I kept quiet on the subject of Betty's past and let Mr Oswald talk.

'Yes,' Mr Oswald tipped his head at me, 'I looked you up, Mrs Fisher. Your record is quite impressive. I had no idea the woman responsible for bringing down the Godmother was going to be handling this investigation.' He mentioned my most well-known case, one which had made news headlines around the world. I was far from famous, but my face had been published enough times that people recognised me.

'How soon after meeting your father did the first theft occur?'

Tim drifted to a sideboard where he had a decanter of something – whisky, I guessed. Baker would have arranged a team of stewards to move his things from the Platinum Suite down to this one so his possessions would be neatly placed away and there was nothing for him to do except relax.

'Scotch?' he offered.

I declined, saying, 'No, thank you,' and waited to see if he would answer my question.

With two fingers of the dark liquid in a crystal tumbler, he eschewed ice or any other accompaniment and sipped it neat.

'I believe it was the same day,' he replied, settling back against the sideboard so he was leaning on it and facing me. 'She arrived late on Tuesday afternoon,' he muttered, regret or annoyance filling his words. 'That awful laugh of hers, that's what I remember hearing. I thought Tulisa had made a friend and brought her back to the suite, goodness knows she needs to spend time with people her own age. I don't remember the last time I saw her even talking to anyone. She just mopes about the cabin, moaning about being held captive because I made her come on this trip rather than leave her at home with the staff. I figured some sun would do her good.'

'Yes,' I agreed, remembering the pasty-skinned teenager. 'She didn't move out of the Platinum Suite?'

Mr Oswald growled into his glass as he swirled the remaining Scotch and downed it in one.

'No. She said she could be unhappy there just as easily as she could here.'

'There is no Mrs Oswald?' I enquired, hoping it wouldn't prove to be a touchy subject. Was he in the middle of a bitter divorce?

He refilled his glass before answering.

'Cancer. Two years ago.' He didn't need to say any more than that.

In a quiet voice I said, 'I'm sorry for your loss.' Sam echoed my words.

'That's not the reason why Tulisa is the way she is though. She started dying her hair black when she was nine. Then one day there were piercings in her face. She was thirteen and had done them herself. Can you believe that? I keep hoping she will come around, but ...' he tailed off, still staring down into his glass and I realised I had misread him earlier. I saw the overbearing powerbroker that I assumed he had to be, but now he just looked sad and worried – a dad with a difficult daughter, failing to understand her choices and wishing he could find a way to communicate with her.

After a moment of silent contemplation, he put the glass down, the second drink untouched, and pushed himself back to upright.

'Sorry, you're here to talk about the gold-digger stealing jewellery, cash, and probably other highly saleable goods from my father's suite. I remember hearing her laugh on that Tuesday afternoon,' he picked up the thread of what he had been saying earlier, 'but was surprised to find it wasn't someone with Tulisa. My father was coming through the door, and he was quite merry. He rarely drinks, but influenced by the pretty young woman, he had been at the cocktails, paying for Betty and all her friends at the swim up bar on the top deck. I let it go; dad wouldn't have listened to me if I asked him to at that point and I saw no harm in it.'

'What did they do when they returned to the suite?' I wanted to know. I had my notebook out and was making notes.

I got a look that said the answer ought to be obvious.

'They went straight into dad's bedroom and the door closed. I didn't bother to listen at the door, but I doubt they were playing tiddlywinks. I went out to dinner and came back and there was still no sign of dad. Tulisa was in her room as she always is, listening to dark music – the sort that makes teenagers take a rifle to school. I asked her if she had seen her grandfather and got a grunt in reply.'

'Do you believe Miss Ross stayed the night?'

'Probably,' he muttered. 'I don't really care. The point is, when I got up the following morning, I couldn't find the cufflinks I had been wearing the previous evening. I was certain I had put them back in the case I keep all my cufflinks in, but they were nowhere to be seen. Later, I noticed the cash in my wallet seemed a little light. I dismissed it though; at the time I thought I must have paid for something and just forgotten about it.'

'So, Miss Ross was still here when you retired and could have wandered the suite during the night when everyone else was asleep?' I wanted him to confirm it.

'Yes. I would say that was the case. I worked until just after eleven and my father's bedroom door was still closed when I turned off the lights.

'Was she still in the suite in the morning?' I asked, curious to hear whether Betty had left during the night and thus gained free rein to wander the suite and pilfer cash and goods.

Tim shook his head. 'No, she was gone. Dad was in his shower when I found him. Singing. Can you believe that? I don't think I have ever heard my father sing before. Not since I was a boy, at least. You're going to ask what he said about the missing money and whether he knew what time she left or if she was up in the night.'

I nodded to confirm those were exactly my next questions.

'Dad didn't know what time she had left, and he didn't care. There was a big, red lip print on his pillow, kind of like a calling card, and beneath it was her mobile phone number and an instruction to call her. I took a photograph.'

Mr Oswald produced a phone from a trouser pocket, his fingers zipping and jabbing at the screen until he turned it around to show me the picture.

'Dad was besotted; I don't know what other term to use, and she was acting just the same as him, pretending that he was her dream man so she could keep him floating along on a ridiculous cloud of passion and perfume while she robbed us. I told him he was acting like a teenager, and he said he just didn't care. Mostly, what had been stolen was easily replaced or it was cash in small amounts, a few thousand dollars is all. I had already argued with dad about it, and it just wasn't worth the hassle to start again. But then the necklace went, and when I checked Tulisa's jewellery – not that she ever wears it, it's not dark enough or something – she had missing items she couldn't account for too. I let it go; I had bigger things to deal with. That is until I noticed my wife's necklace was missing.'

'Did you confront her?'

'No.' He was muttering under his breath, unhappy at how he had handled the matter and wishing he had a second chance to get it right. 'No, I confronted my father. When I got up that morning,' he cast his eyes up into his skull to consult his memory, 'she had already left the suite; a thief in the night sneaking out with nary a care for the victims of her crime. I found dad though and we got into a fight about it. He insisted she would never do such a thing; as if he knew her. I blew my top and it's been a downhill train ride from there. Dad promised me he would speak to her about it, but two days went by, and he was still looking for the right opportunity. Then we docked in Gibraltar and a whole load more of my wife's jewellery, a Patek Phillippe watch, and some of my daughter's things all vanished.'

No wonder Betty's next visit to the suite had provoked such a strong reaction from him.

'Well, you witnessed what happened this morning. I told dad he had one last shot to make her give back the things she had taken, or I was getting the ship's security team involved. I should have contacted your team earlier, of course.' He tutted at himself. 'When I woke up this morning to find even more cash missing, I blew my stack. I stormed into dad's room, and well ... your team arrived a little while later.'

We talked a while longer, but I learned nothing new. The missing jewellery and cash had started to disappear almost as soon as Betty Ross walked through the door to the Platinum Suite. It was circumstantial, but nevertheless believable. She was a woman of little means, she had no job and had lied about it, and she had a history of stealing if her mother was to be taken at face value.

I saw no reason to doubt the very obvious conclusion staring me in the face. Betty Ross was a gold-digging strumpet and probably assuming the gravy train she was riding would end soon was stashing trinkets to keep herself going.

Catching her was going to be fun.

Just as I was wrapping things up with Tim Oswald, my phone began to ring. I begged a moment, checked the screen, and handed it to Sam.

'It's Lieutenant Bhukari,' I let him know. 'Please see what she wants.'

Before I could conclude matters with Mr Oswald, Sam said, 'She says Mrs Purcell just left her suite. We should come quickly.'

My nostrils flared as I sucked in a sudden breath. 'Right. Tell her we're on our way. No, wait,' I gestured urgently for the phone, nodded a goodbye to Mr Oswald and started toward his door to leave. 'Are you in?' I asked her.

Acting Shady

'Um, no, Mrs Fisher,' Deepa replied uncertainly. 'Martin thought it better to wait until you were available. He's near her cabin with Pippin. Schneider and I have been tailing Mrs Purcell.'

Right. My team was still trying to get used to my somewhat slack attitude towards some of the rules we were expected to obey. How were we expected to conduct an investigation if we couldn't look where we wanted to look? Especially when we wanted to look somewhere that the passenger involved might not want us to look? If we asked Priscilla for permission to enter her cabin, she was going to say no or sanitise it to make sure there was nothing left to find.

'Where is Mrs Purcell now?' I asked.

Deepa's voice echoed back, 'With a gaggle of other ladies at the coffee place on deck eighteen. They are having tea and cakes and it looks like she just told them about her sister. They look shocked.'

Evelyn and Priscilla were travelling as a pair, so the other ladies would be people they had met since coming on board. It happened like that, passengers gravitating towards other passengers because they spoke the same language and were of a similar age.

'It might be worth making a note of who they are,' I remarked, expecting that would now happen. 'Let us know the moment she leaves the table.'

Ending the call, I turned to my assistant. 'Come along, Sam. We have to do something sneaky.'

Sam chuckled, hurrying along beside me as we raced to the nearest elevator. I wasn't worried about getting caught; the likelihood was very low. Priscilla would take ten minutes or more to return from where she was, and I would have advance warning – something sadly lacking the first few times I snuck into other people's cabins with a liberated universal key card.

Using Sam's radio because I forgot to pick mine up again, I contacted Baker.

'Mrs Fisher,' he got straight to the point. 'Are you on your way to Mrs Purcell's cabin?'

I skirted around the question. 'Is there anyone around?'

'No, it's all quiet here.'

It was what I expected. There is nothing to do in one's cabin and so much to do and see everywhere else on the ship. Passengers only went back to their cabin during the day if they needed something.

'Okay, toss the place. Remember you are looking for an undetectable poison or some chemicals or medicines that could be used to stop Evelyn's heart. If Priscilla killed her sister, then she is a wily one and might have already gotten rid of what she used.'

'You're not coming?' Baker asked, sounding nervous suddenly. 'I'm not entirely comfortable entering her cabin like this.'

Strange how he was okay for me to do it though.

'No, Martin,' I answered. 'I know the justification for searching her cabin is tenuous and she just lost her sister. Nevertheless, we need to know what there is to know and we already know she is acting shady.'

'Where are you going to be, Mrs Fisher?' he asked.

I huffed a breath, accepting my latest crazy plan as precisely that, but content it would quickly get me what I wanted.

‘I’ll be playing dressing up.’

Stop! Thief!

After a swift call to Deepa to confirm a few things and let her know what I planned, I stopped off at a boutique on deck nineteen – I knew just what I had to buy. I grabbed what I needed and swiped my card. It was a minor expense, especially if I was able to pull off the fast-hand act I pictured in my head.

I suppose you could say I learned it from the passport thieves, but their act of grab, swap, swap which ensured the victim wouldn't be able to find their wallet or purse no matter what, wouldn't work for me because Priscilla knew my face.

To pull this off, I needed a disguise.

I also needed a third person.

Jermaine reluctantly agreed.

'We are actually stealing her handbag, madam?' he sought to confirm.

'Borrowing,' I corrected him. 'You can think of it as doing her a service if you like. We are going to take her bag, look through it, and give it back.'

It hadn't taken Baker and Pippin long to call me back to say there was nothing to find in Priscilla's cabin. They emptied her bin and checked in her drawers and in the cabinet above the sink. My undetectable poison was proving elusive.

Unperturbed by the lack of success so far, I was hoping my next tactic would change the tide.

It took me a few minutes to get ready, the makeup and hair hard to get right. I used pictures from an internet search on my phone to guide my hands, but after a few attempts I decided I looked sufficiently not like me.

'Wow,' said Sam.

Jermaine showed me the white around his pupils as his eyes almost popped out of his head.

Yup, I had the outfit about right. To throw Priscilla off my scent, I was dressed just like Tulisa had been earlier. I bought a black hair dye, one of those spray on things that washes out straight away in water, and a large can of hairspray to mess my hair up and make it look like I had just been having vigorous sex with a kangaroo. My outfit was black and grungy. At least, I called it grungy but would have to admit that I don't really know what that word means.

'I just need to borrow some boots from Barbie. Do you know if she has anything chunky with lots of laces?' I asked Jermaine.

He had changed out of his butler's livery upon my request and was now wearing a grey suit with a pink pinstripe running through it. He didn't know what I might find in Barbie's wardrobe though so I went to look, certain my friend wouldn't mind.

I didn't find what I wanted, not exactly, but I did find a pair of boots that would finish the outfit. They were thigh high and laced at the back with a blocky heel but where Tulisa had worn boots that one might more typically find on a construction worker, the ones Barbie had belonged in a brothel. I had never seen her in them so could only speculate that she wore them for Hideki and no one else.

'Those belong to Barbie?' asked Sam, his eyes out on stalks when I tottered out of her bedroom.

'Yes, why?' I gave Sam a sideways look, never sure what might be going through his head.

'No reason,' he replied coyly. 'I saw some ladies wearing boots like that in a magazine once. My uncle had them hidden under his bed when we went to stay at his house.'

I could feel the heat rising off my cheeks.

'Yes, well, I'm sure Barbie just wears them when she wants to do dressing up.'

Jermaine nodded. 'U-huh. That's exactly what she wears them for.'

My blush deepened another shade.

'Are we ready?' I asked, changing the subject.

Jermaine picked up his umbrella. 'Tell me again why you need to employ such a radical tactic, madam?' he requested, setting his feet, and looking like he might not move unless I convinced him to.

I let my shoulders drop, feeling that time was of the essence because Priscilla would finish her lunch and want to move on soon, but also knowing I needed Jermaine on board for this to work and he deserved to go into such a risky task fully informed.

'There have been some complaints about me,' I revealed, following up by explaining precisely what that meant and could mean. 'Yes, you could argue that getting caught snatching a passenger's bag when I have no legitimate right to demand to search it is encouraging Purple Star to can the whole ship's detective idea, but they are just as likely to scrap my job if I don't start solving crimes.'

Jermaine dipped his head in a dutiful salute.

'I am always to be found at your side, madam.' He always found the best things to say, and I felt my bottom lip wobble as the pressure of the situation and the anger I felt over the unjust complaints bubbled to the surface. Just having Jermaine in my life made it so much richer.

I shoved it back down, steeling my resolve. Hiding the hand that swiped away the single tear escaping my right eye by scooping the dogs to put them on their favourite couch, I kissed them both goodbye, getting wet noses to my face in response.

Back on my feet, I said, 'Let's do it.'

My phone rang. It was Deepa and she wasn't using the radio because she didn't need anyone else to find themselves on our channel and listening in to my dubious decisions.

'They just got the check, Mrs Fisher, are you here?'

'No,' I whined. 'I'm only just leaving my cabin. Is there a way to delay them?'

There was a pause before Deepa answered. 'I can try to hold up the waiter. I'll, um. I'll bat my eyes at him.'

Unless he was gay that was going to work just fine, Deepa was a young, athletic, and above all, attractive woman. A smile from her would stop most men in their tracks.

There was no time for us to lose though, so we hustled, Sam in his Ensign's uniform, Jermaine dressed like John Steed from *The Avengers*, and me dressed as Siouxsie Sioux's battered aunt. We had to look like the strangest trio, and we sure turned some heads on our way to intercept Priscilla.

Would we be fast enough to get there before the old ladies finished their tea and cake and split up to do whatever they had planned next?

No. We wouldn't.

The call from Deepa came just as we arrived at the coffee house.

'Sorry, Mrs Fisher. The waiter is gay. He asked me to pass his number to Schneider. The ladies have paid, and they are on their way out of the coffee shop right now. How close are you?'

We were right at the doors and about to go inside, that's how close we were. Priscilla was on the other side, about to grab the handle and the only reason she didn't look right at me was because she had her head turned to hear what the lady next to her was saying.

I stifled a squeal of panic and jumped to my left just as the doors opened. The way to my left wasn't exactly clear, there was a display of exotic plants there which I crashed into, toppled, wrestled back to upright with a grunt of effort and then hid behind.

'What was that?' asked Priscilla as she left the coffee shop.

'What was what?' questioned one of her companions.

I could almost hear Priscilla's frown as she peered around the plants, and I crawled away beneath the tables and chairs arranged outside the coffee shop.

Jermaine and Sam, caught in the open, had proceeded inside the coffee shop. Our well-rehearsed grab, swap, swap was up in smoke unless I could get away and get them back into position.

When I felt I was far enough away, I stopped and rolled to my side.

Priscilla and her friends hadn't loitered outside the coffee shop where they would have blocked the entrance, they were ten yards away in the open where they had formed a gaggle once more.

‘Here, what are you doing?’ asked a voice from behind me.

I had come up into a crouch and was peering around a chair to watch my target but had failed to notice the people sitting in the coffee shop’s outdoor area.

The voice belonged to a man in his late twenties. His accent was Jamaican, if my ears were any good, but it could have easily been any of the other Caribbean islands from which he hailed. His hair was reduced to a tight buzzcut, and he had a military look about him which is to say he had muscle beneath his t-shirt, and an air of ready-to-mix-it-up.

Stumbling for words, I said, ‘Um, I dropped a contact lens. Here it is.’ I mimed picking something up and pretended to put it in my eye the way I had seen people do. Unfortunately, not only did he look like he didn’t believe me, but I managed to poke myself in the eye with what was now a dirty finger covered in grime and dust from the deck.

I stood up, feeling an urgent need to move away from the young man who was now eyeing me with deep suspicion. Priscilla was moving away, splitting off from her friends as she walked in a different direction to the rest of them.

I questioned where she might be going and if I could grab Sam and Jermaine before she escaped our sight, but with a gasp, a new opportunity presented itself.

She was heading for the ladies’ restroom.

Still rubbing at my eye, and planning to wash it out with a little water, I made a beeline for the same place. I slowed my pace, giving Priscilla enough time to get inside and find a stall.

I needed luck on my side – I couldn't do anything if there were ladies hanging around nattering and touching up their makeup inside, but the one woman who was in there washing her hands and checking her face, left while I was splashing water into my eye.

She gave me a disapproving look in the mirror, breaking eye contact the moment I saw her looking my way. It was my outfit and hair that did it. Or so I thought.

When I looked back at my reflection, checking to see if my eye was red, I discovered that the water I had flicked at my face had gone on my hair as well. It had mixed with the dye and was running out of my hairline and into my eyebrows.

It looked like my brain was leaking!

I gasped, rubbing at the inky black liquid seeping across my forehead but that just made it worse. My fingers tracking through it made it look like I had a tyre tread pattern above my eyebrows. My head had been run over by a car.

I was a mess for sure, but the restroom, with the exception of whoever was in the stalls, was empty. My heart thudded in my chest. If I was going to do this, it had to be right now.

Bent at the waist, I peered along the line of stalls – there were feet visible under three of the doors, but only one set of shoes that could be Priscilla's. I doubted she was wearing red high heels or a set of Gucci sling backs which I rather fancied a pair of for myself.

Pricilla's handbag was right next to her sensible flat shoes, placed on the floor and within easy reach if I ducked down in the stall next to hers.

Eight seconds later, with Priscilla shouting at the top of her lungs, I hit the door to the restroom and burst through it.

Straight into the arms of the young Jamaican man.

Fishy Situation

Only the speed at which I was moving saved me. I checked into his body, slamming the air from his lungs as he went over backwards. I got a glimpse of Jermaine's tall figure standing next to the white uniforms of Sam, Deepa, and Schneider. They were in front of the coffee shop and clearly looking for me. Deepa's phone was at her ear and my phone started ringing before I could draw another breath

Of course, Jermaine and the others were all looking my way by then as was everyone else in a thirty-yard radius.

The restroom door was still swinging shut, Priscilla's outraged cries of 'Help, thief! Somebody just stole my bag!' were too loud to be missed.

I scrambled to my feet, fighting to get traction in Barbie's silly sex boots and only narrowly missed being caught by the man I knocked over as his hands flailed to grab a handful of my clothes.

One last panicked glance in Jermaine's direction allowed me to see him say something colourful and then I was running as fast as I could. I was the ship's detective, on board to act as a deterrent to anyone thinking of committing a crime and there to investigate whenever anyone did.

How was it that I had just stolen a lady's handbag?

Now, I may have mentioned it before, but I am not the world's fastest runner. At fifty-three, whatever speed I had when I was younger, has escaped me, so even though it felt like I was running like the wind, I knew it wouldn't take long for someone to catch me. The question at the centre of my mind was who would it be.

Priscilla's handbag was tucked under my left arm like a rugby ball as I pumped the air with my right. My breath started to catch in my throat before I had gone twenty yards, but there was a bank of elevators ahead. If I timed it right, I might be able to get into one and get away clean.

No such luck. I got a few yards closer and could see both cars were decks away from me. Shouts from behind me filled the air as people gave pursuit and I could pick out the voice of the young Jamaican man as he bellowed for me to stop.

I wove between startled passengers, aiming for the doors that would take me out and onto the sundeck. I had to think about what deck I was on and where that would place me in comparison to everything else. Out of breath and driven by fear, my brain wouldn't do the math, so I put my shoulder down and careened through the doors and out into the sun.

I don't know how many women have ever tried running in heels, I mean properly running, but I'm willing to bet it's not many. If you were wearing heels and had to run for your life, you would just kick them off, wouldn't you? Well, that's not an option with thigh-length boots, so I was running on my toes and really struggling to stay on my feet.

The sun deck was busy, people in their swimsuits blocked my path in every direction like a wall of flesh.

I screamed, 'Get out of my way!' running directly for a gaggle of men and women waiting in line for drinks at one of the bars. If I could lose my chasers here, I could hide out in one of the changing rooms, heck, maybe I could even swipe a bathing suit and change my appearance. If they were looking for a woman all in black, with stupid boots, and a stolen handbag, I would give them bikini girl. A hat could cover my hair if I could find one of those unattended.

As my list of things to steal got longer and I realised what I was thinking of doing would only make things worse, I heard the same door I had come through a moment ago slam back against its stops and risked a glance over my shoulder.

It was the Jamaican man again!

I jinked right, knowing I could go behind the bars at the far end of the pool and into the changing rooms located on the other side. I had a lead, and he would be hampered by having to go around people just the same as I was. I could make it.

Except he decided to cheat.

Effortlessly, the young man altered his course and ran across a line of sunbeds. They didn't fold up and smack him in the bum the same way they did to me when I chased the Turkish passport thieves. Oh no, they acted as a springboard for him, accelerating his pace as he cut across at an angle instead of going around the obstacles as I knew I had to do.

I heard him coming, his rage-filled war cry heard by everyone as he launched off the final sunbed to hit me with a flying tackle.

Had I slammed into the deck it would have hurt like hell, but instead of that, for the second time in two days, I went into the pool.

I let go of the bag, or rather, it was ejected from my grip, and as I pitched backward into the water, I got to see a surprised lady on a sunbed catch it. I also saw Buddy the Gibraltar Rock Ape. He was skulking in a shady corner where he was eating a piece of pineapple he had probably taken from someone's empty cocktail glass. I saw him look my way, then I was under water and fighting to get back to the surface.

There wasn't enough air in my lungs for me to hold my breath and I was under for far too long. When I finally came up for air, I was gasping and retching, trying to get air into my lungs and wondering if I was going to pass out.

Hands gripped my arms and there were more people jumping into the pool. I could barely see, the dye from my hair was running over my face and into my eyes, but I could hear.

'I saw her,' the Jamaican man reported. 'I saw her watching someone and then she followed her into the ladies' restroom. I knew she was up to no good.'

'Thank you, Sir, we'll take it from here,' replied a voice I knew.

'Schneider?' I gasped between heaving breaths.

I got an insistent, 'Shhhh!' from Deepa who was right behind me and taking my left arm in a vice-like grip. 'You are under arrest for theft, destruction of property, and ... errr, wilful contamination of a swimming pool.'

I wiped a little water out of my eyes with the one free hand I had and squinted at the water. It looked like someone had slaughtered a whole bunch of squid in it. All around me there was a spreading oil slick of black dye from my hair. Was there any left on my head?

The Jamaican man was being ushered out of the pool by Bhukari and Schneider who were in the water with me and taking control.

The man who tackled me got a round of applause while I got whispered at to keep my hair over my face and keep my eyes looking down. Bhukari and Schneider were going to get me away from the situation, but I had to play along.

'Move aside please, everyone,' Schneider requested. 'We need to get this one to the brig.'

'Wait one moment.' The commanding voice stopped everyone dead in their tracks and my heart simply gave up trying to beat.

Alistair was here.

There was a spray of water to my left as the soaking wet Lieutenant Schneider cracked out a crisp salute.

'Sir. We just caught this one attempting to flee the scene after snatching a lady's handbag, Sir. It's a very fishy situation, sir,' he added in a not-so-subtle attempt to tell him what was going on.

I wanted the ground to open up beneath me. Or maybe they could just chuck me overboard. I was good with either.

Alistair wasn't picking up on the obvious clues though.

'Am I to understand that you were the one to give pursuit and catch the criminal?' he asked, turning his attention to the Jamaican man.

'That's right, mon,' he replied in his island lilt. 'I could see she was up to no good.'

'Lieutenant Commander Baker,' Alistair addressed the next senior crew member at the scene as he arrived at a run with Lieutenant Pippin right on his shoulder. 'Make a note of this passenger's name and cabin number.' He turned his attention back to the Jamaican man. 'Well done, Sir. I am the captain of this fine vessel and shall see to it that you are suitably honoured for your efforts. Are you travelling with company?'

The man turned to his left, aiming a soaking wet arm at the young woman who had been with him at the coffee shop.

'This is my wife. We are travelling home after our honeymoon.'

‘Congratulations to you both,’ Alistair beamed as if proud they had selected the Aurelia for their homeward leg. ‘I believe we shall start with an upgrade to one of our suites on deck nineteen.’

The couple were shocked and over the moon with the unexpected boon, and I realised then what Alistair was doing. He knew it was me and was making sure the crowd’s attention was pointing elsewhere.

Extending an arm to guide the couple back inside the ship’s superstructure, Alistair nodded his head at Baker.

‘Take that one away, Lieutenant Commander.’ He paused though before he walked away, changing his mind to cross the space between us. Leaning to get closer to me, but not touching for fear I might ruin his uniform too, he said, ‘I rather like those boots. Maybe you can wear them later to make up for this.’

He delivered his suggestion in a bedroom voice and immediately rejoined the Jamaican couple as my cheeks reddened.

2200

We hustled to get away from the sundeck, Lieutenant Commander Baker leading the way and requesting people make space so that the soggier lieutenants still holding my arms could walk me through the crowd.

Sam and Jermaine were with us, tagging on behind until we were away from other passengers and could speak.

'Jermaine,' Baker addressed him first. 'I think we probably need to get Mrs Fisher cleaned up and dressed before we take her back to her suite just in case anyone sees where she goes. We'll take her down to the operations room. Can you meet us there?'

With a dip of his head, Jermaine departed, and the rest of us got into an elevator.

'Are your uniforms going to be okay?' I asked, pushing my lank locks of black hair out of my face. Both Bhukari and Schneider looked a state, their pristine whites now grey and stained.

Deepa lifted an arm to inspect it.

'No, probably not. They can give us new ones though.'

'That's easy for you to say,' moaned Schneider. 'They don't carry them in my size. I have to have them made.'

'You have spares,' Baker pointed out. 'More importantly, what is in the handbag?'

Sam had the handbag – he'd retrieved it from under a sun lounger while I was going for a swim. No doubt Priscilla was somewhere up on the sundeck, questioning what had happened to it. We could get it back to her soon enough, but I wanted to see what was in it first. It needed to be something good, considering the trouble I had gone to.

We fell upon the task there and then, emptying the contents of the handbag onto the floor of the elevator car. Phone, tissues, a tatty romance novel, a purse containing notes from several different countries and some pocket change, plus the usual paraphernalia and credit cards. However, there was no smoking gun. There wasn't a gun of any kind for that matter. I was hoping there might be a syringe or a clever little phial containing the exotic undetectable drug she had used to kill her sister. The closest we got was a half-used packet of paracetamol.

'And there was nothing in her cabin?' I begged Baker and Pippin with a sigh.

Baker gave a sorry shake of his head, mirrored by Lieutenant Pippin's apologetic expression.

'There was certainly nothing hidden anywhere to indicate that she was trying to prevent people finding it. The cabinet in her cabin's bathroom just held regular toiletries. Her room had just been cleaned though ...'

I cut him off midsentence. 'How recently?'

Baker's eyes widened slightly at the intensity of my stare.

'Um, the cleaner was still going down the passageway,' he admitted. 'That wasn't all that long ago, He's probably only got another couple of cabins along.'

'Then we need to get back up there and see if he found anything when he was tidying the room,' I insisted. 'We are missing something ... I have no idea what it is, but there is something vital that I don't understand about Evelyn's death and her sister knows what it is. I need to find a clue that I can use to force her to tell me what it is.'

Baker pressed the button to stop the elevator at the next deck.

'Pippin and I will go straight back up there,' he announced as the elevator slowed.

As he was getting off, his wife, Deepa Bhukari, announced that she had worked around the passcode on Priscilla's phone.

'It's a simple six-digit code,' she remarked, her fingers tapping at the screen to open different apps. 'Lots of people use their birthdays – month and year. I just looked hers up on central registry, but it wasn't that, she had used her sister's instead.'

I was thankful to have a good team of people around me, it would have taken me a year to open her phone.

Frowning down at the device, Deepa revealed, 'There's not much here. She's had a couple of calls and just a handful of messages in the last two weeks. They all match up to entries in her contacts apart from this one.'

We crowded around her, getting up close to her shoulders so we could see what was on the screen. There was a number displayed at the top, but no name, and the message contained only four digits.

2200

'Does that mean anything to anyone?' I asked, looking around hopefully.

'Is it the time?' Sam asked.

'It could be,' I acknowledged, not wanting to dissuade anyone from shouting out ideas.

Deepa was frowning again. 'My first guess would be a cabin number, but we don't have a cabin with that number to the best of my knowledge.'

Schneider shook his head. 'It's not a cabin,' he stated confidently. 'I think that's a room down in engineering on deck two.'

'Deck two?' Deepa and I echoed in unison.

'Why would anybody be messaging Priscilla about deck two? Or anything below the passenger decks, for that matter?' I wasn't asking them to supply an answer, and nobody had one anyway.

We were drawing a surprising number of blanks in this case, and it was beginning to irk me.

The elevator stopped, spitting us out on deck ten so we could go to our operations room. Once inside, and with the world shut outside, I held out my hand for Deepa to give me Priscilla's phone.

'You're going to call the number?' she guessed correctly.

I took the phone and thumbed the button to call the unknown number. I also put it onto speaker, so we could all hear.

It rang for several seconds before a man's voice filled our operations room.

'Hey, baby, you want more?'

I opened my mouth to speak, questioned whether I could pull off Priscilla's voice and accepted that I was going to have to try.

'I really do,' I replied, keeping it short and hoping we might learn something.

Instead, the line went dead, the man at the other end able to identify that I wasn't who he expected to hear.

I muttered a rude word before focusing on what we had just learned.

'Okay, so the mysterious message came from a man, and he sounded pleased to be hearing from Priscilla.' I walked across the operations room to one of the whiteboards, snatching up a marker to write first the four digits of the message at the top, and then the words he had said beneath it.

Stepping back, everyone could see, 'Hey, baby, you want more?' and a little line to join up to where I had written *man's voice*.

'He sounded European,' Schneider stated.

Deepa nodded her head, 'He did,' she agreed. 'I'm not too good with European accents though,' she admitted. 'I don't think I could pin it down any better than that, but he didn't sound like you,' she pointed out with a nod in Schneider's direction to make it clear who she was talking about.

'No, that wasn't a German or Austrian accent,' I agreed. 'How about Spanish?'

We all looked at each other until Sam chipped in his thoughts, 'He sounded Italian to me,' and then proceeded to demonstrate what he thought an Italian accent sounded like by repeating the somewhat awful accents employed on a well-known series of television advertisements for a famous brand of Italian sauce.

It drew a smile from the rest of us and on the board, I wrote 'Italian' and put a question mark after it.

A polite knock on the door to the operations room turned out to be Jermaine returning. He had clothing for me, towels, make up, and a hat to hide my hair. There was nowhere to get changed so I was just going to have to get on and do it where I was, protecting my modesty by using the towels efficiently. Not that anyone was going to try to ogle me of course, but equally, I didn't plan to just drop my drawers in the middle of the room.

Retreating to a corner, I began unbuttoning my top.

'I think perhaps Schneider and I should take this opportunity to go and change our clothing too,' Deepa suggested, thumping the tall Austrian on his arm to get him moving towards the door. She was giving me space, of course, but as Schneider opened the door, Baker and Pippin came back through it.

They were carrying bags of trash - several of them, which they deposited on the floor against the far wall.

Taking his hat off and scratching his head while he stared down at the mound of bags, Baker said, 'We got there just in time to stop this lot going down the chute to the compactor in the hold. But we're gonna have to sift through it to see if there is anything here worth finding.'

Before any of us could question the fruitless nature of such an attempt, Pippin added, 'The cleaner said he picked up something from beneath Mrs Purcell's bed. It was a scrap of paper.'

Sinking to his knees, Baker selected the first of four bags of trash and began taking pieces out.

'It's probably going to prove to be nothing, even if we can find it,' he sighed. 'Nevertheless ...'

Pippin was just about to join him when he noticed the new notation on the whiteboard. His query about it led to a brief discussion of the very short phone call with the possibly Italian man.

'Ricardo Rossini is Italian,' Lieutenant Pippin pointed out.

Baker, Bhukari, Schneider, Sam, and Jermaine all looked at him and then at me.

'Who's Ricardo Rossini?'

They all asked the question at more or less the same time, and I did my best to explain about the man Lieutenant Pippin had seen with both sisters several hours before Evelyn died. I also explained that he was staying on board with his husband.

I concluded by saying, 'Clearly, it is now time we investigated his possible involvement.'

Deepa and Schneider made good their escape, returning to their cabins in the crew area to get cleaned up and into fresh uniforms. Lieutenant Commander Baker elected himself to be the one to return Priscilla's handbag to her, leaving Pippin and Sam to the laborious task of sifting trash, though Baker promised to be back shortly.

I got changed out of my soggy clothes, the boots I borrowed from Barbie popping off my feet with a squelching, sucking noise. I was going to have to apologise to her, firstly for taking them without seeking her permission, but also then for ruining them. I would replace them of course, and I hoped in seeking her out to apologise I could broach the subject of what was bothering her.

Once dressed in dry clothing and able to move around the ship without danger of being identified as the person who had just attempted to steal

Priscilla's bag, I left Pippin and Sam sifting the trash and went back to my suite to get cleaned up properly.

I still had black dye in my hair that needed to come out.

There's a Bug

It took three goes with the shampoo before I was content the dye had gone, and I was in the shower for long enough that when I emerged the room was full of steam, and I was a surprising shade of pink all over.

Dressed in a soft towelling robe, I settled at my dressing table and questioned what the heck I was doing. I was so shaken and off balance because of the stupid complaints that I wasn't thinking straight. I could have been caught with Priscilla's handbag, really caught, that is, not just apprehended by my own team.

Word of my escapade would not get out, Baker and the others would see to that, and thank goodness because there were members of the crew who did not approve of me. One, who was quite vocal in his opinion, was Commander Philips, the head of engineering who I had a run in with while posing as a crew member the day he came on board.

Alistair came to my rescue on that occasion, and I got the impression Commander Philips was still smarting from the encounter. Pushing the jarring memory of my poor decisions to one side, I refocussed on the two cases I was working on.

Then my phone rang, displaying Hideki's name to remind me that I had a third case to keep me occupied – that of the murdered stowaway.

My phone was on the bed, a foot from my dachshunds who must have chosen to get up there while I was in the shower.

Georgie had lifted her head and was eyeing it with a puppy-sized frown – the infernal thing had woken her. She dropped her head back to the covers and closed her eyes when I picked it up.

'Hello, Hideki.' I was looking at my reflection in the long mirror behind my dressing table.

Did I have another wrinkle coming by my right eye? That wasn't there yesterday!

Hideki was talking, but my attention was on my face where I was using my fingers to stretch my skin to remove the wrinkle. Reaching for my super expensive ceramide night cream and wondering if I should sleep with my face plunged into the tub, I kind of knew Hideki was talking, but I hadn't taken anything in.

With a small sigh, he repeated himself.

'I said I found a bug in the man's hair – the stowaway. He had a small dead bug in the matted hair behind his left ear.'

I screwed up my face in disgust, both for the bug and the fact that the man's hair was so dirty he hadn't noticed it was in there.

'I didn't recognise it, so I sent a picture to an old buddy of mine from college. I went to med school, and he went into entomology. It turns out that the bug is super rare, so rare in fact that it only exists on one island. It's in the Mediterranean approximately ten miles off the coast of North Africa. It's called Asreb and is part of the autonomous city of Melilla.'

I scrunched up my head, trying to remember my geography classes.

'That's Spanish, right?'

'Right,' Hideki confirmed. 'Whoever he is, it's highly likely that he was on that island in the days before his death. I thought you would want to know. Barbie always says you find a way to add the clues together to find the answers no one else can.'

'Yes, thank you,' I replied absentmindedly, my brain whizzing off on a tangent already. Snapping back to reality for a second, I asked, 'Hey, how's things with Barbie? Are you guys doing okay?' I was prying, but there was clearly something bothering her.

'Yeah, sure,' Hideki replied, then his tone changed. 'Why? Did she say something? Did I forget her birthday or ...'

'No, no, it's nothing like that,' I cut him off before he could start to worry. 'It's probably just me. I haven't seen her much recently and I wanted to check everything was all right.'

Hideki sounded uncertain when he replied, 'So far as I know, everything is hunky dory.' The expression sounded odd in his Japanese accent. 'I'm having dinner with her later, so I can ask.'

'No, please! Please, it's probably nothing and she's so fiercely independent, she will want to work it out for herself if there is anything.'

Hideki agreed. 'You're not wrong. Well, I called to tell you about the bug. Do you think maybe that is where the jewels came from?'

I shrugged even though he couldn't see the gesture.

'I couldn't possibly say, Hideki. I'll need a little more to go on, but at least we have something to tell the authorities now.'

With the call ended, I did my best to not obsess over the wrinkle and forced myself away from the mirror to look for clothes. I selected a loose pair of slacks in a tan colour, combining them with a pair of Mary Janes with a low heel, and a cream blouse on top that did a great job of hiding my less-than-toned middle. I wouldn't normally be conscious of such a thing, but living with Barbie, who couldn't possibly come up with a part of her body she didn't like, I found myself comparing bits of me with bits of her.

I know, I know, she's got thirty years on me. It's silly, but I do it anyway.

With my blonde friend on my mind, I left my bedroom with the dachshunds on my heels – they were after a biscuit. I was going to the upper deck gym to find her. I was right about her being independent, but reinforcing that I was there if she needed to talk couldn't hurt, right?

'Do you need anything before you depart, madam?' asked Jermaine, making me jump when he appeared unexpectedly from the lobby area of my suite. He had a hand steamer in his grip.

I twisted around, cringing away from the perceived danger. The dogs just looked at me – I guess they knew he was there.

'Jermaine, do you have to do that?' I snapped as my heart restarted.

'I was removing the creases from your coats, madam,' he explained. 'I apologise for alarming you.'

'You're too quiet,' I complained. 'Try humming sometimes, please.'

He dipped his head. 'As you wish, madam.'

I sagged and hung my head. 'I wasn't being kind, Jermaine. I'm sorry. Today has been ... it's been a little trying.'

'Is there anything I can do to be of assistance?' he asked. 'I am at your disposal regardless of the task.'

I walked over to him, putting a hand on his arm.

'You do too much already, Jermaine. I couldn't function without you.' I hoped he knew how true that was. I looked up into his big, brown eyes and a moment passed between us. We had been through a lot, and we did it together. There was a bond that could never be broken.

I looked away before mushiness could occur.

'I have to get on. I'll take the girls,' I looked down to find the dachshunds wagging their tails at me. They knew I was going out. 'I am heading for the Platinum Suite if anyone comes calling.'

A few moments later I was in the passageway outside my suite with the sun streaming through the panoramic windows to remind me where I was. The view beyond was nothing but sea. We were out of the Mediterranean and sailing down the coast of Africa on our way to the Canary Islands.

I turned my feet to face in the opposite direction to the one that would take me to the Oswalds' Suite – I was going to see Barbie first.

Angry Friend

I found her easily enough, she was leading a class in the gym, just where I knew she would be. Standing at the front and facing the sweaty, pain-stricken fools who signed up to have the blonde bombshell torture them, Barbie had a barbell above her head and was yelling into the microphone of her headset as she squatted to the floor and back up again several times.

My plan was to wait, out of the way in the corner of the class - I wasn't in anyone's way and had done this a dozen times before when I needed to speak to her. So it was to my great surprise when she turned her head to yell in my direction.

'No spectators! And no pets in the gym! Join in or be gone!'

My mouth hung open. This wasn't the Barbie I knew. Any question that something was bothering her went out of the window – she was upset and angry and she was aiming it at me. I could not fathom why. I could not come up with anything I could have done that might have upset her. Yet, she was flicking her eyes my way to see if I was moving yet as she barked another order at her class.

Unable to think of anything else I could do, I grabbed the door handle, mouthed, 'Sorry,' in her direction and slipped back out into the gym's reception area.

One of her colleagues was there, a muscular, black man in his early thirties called Derrick.

'Everything all right, Mrs Fisher?' he asked, looking up from his computer.

I smiled and lied, 'Yes, all good. I wanted to speak to Barbie, but she's busy right now.'

'She'll be finished soon. Do you want to hang on?' he asked.

I shook my head. 'No, it's nothing important.' It really was. 'I'll catch up with her later.' Like when I have had a chance to grill Jermaine and Hideki and find out what was going on.

I thanked Derrick and waved goodbye in an overly exuberant way as I tried to compensate for how off balance I felt. First the complaints and now Barbie was upset with me.

Telling myself whatever it was would just be a silly misunderstanding and we would be hugging it out before I knew it, I pushed on to my next destination. I was heading for John Oswald's suite – there was an investigation to conduct, and I was yet to talk to half of the people involved.

Okay, so John's granddaughter, Tulisa, probably wouldn't have much to say, such being her general attitude to life, but I would not be doing my job if I didn't attempt to glean what knowledge she might hold. She was a victim too, it seemed, some of her jewellery going missing when the other items vanished.

The butler, Bartholomew, a dapper man in his fifties, thin as a rake and as English as a crumpet being eaten by the Queen, answered the door.

'Hello, Bartholomew,' I offered him a warm smile I really wasn't feeling.

'Ah, Mrs Fisher,' he replied, his tone devoid of emotion - he was about as butlery as a butler could get. 'Are you here to speak with Mr Oswald Senior?'

'Yes, please?'

'Who is it?' the voice of John Oswald echoed out from somewhere in the suite.

I knew Bartholomew would want to formally announce me, but I didn't give him the chance.

'It's Patricia Fisher,' I called over the butler's head, much to his annoyance. Not that he showed it in anything other than a slight tightening of his eyes. 'The ship's detective.'

A sense of someone moving became John Oswald a second later when he appeared behind Bartholomew.

'Yes, I was expecting you to return sooner or later. I guess it's sooner. Please, come in.'

Bartholomew stepped backward and to one side to let me in, the dogs shooting forward to get inside and explore.

'Dogs too,' John commented.

'Is that okay?' I enquired, pausing because I had been about to ask if I could let them off the lead.

He nodded. 'Yes. I'm a dog person. My Tim had one when he was a boy,' John reminisced.

I let the dogs go, the pair of them scampering under a couch before emerging on the other side and running around somewhere behind it, out of sight.

'Yes, he told me when I visited him,' I remarked, easing into a conversation.

John asked, 'How is he?' and it surprised me that it was his first question. I could hear the concern in his voice.

Meeting his gaze head on, I said, 'Unhappy with how things have transpired, I believe. I cannot speak for him, but I believe he regrets his outburst.' John nodded, opting to watch the dogs sniffing around rather than looking at me. 'Nevertheless, I have to believe that the jewellery and cash he reports missing have, in fact, been stolen, and I am duty-bound to investigate it.'

Now he met my eyes. 'Betty didn't take it. She has no reason to.'

'You sound very certain,' I challenged him.

His eyebrows jumped a little, before settling into a frown that threatened a rebuke. It passed as quickly as it came, John Oswald slumping a little as he accepted my point was valid.

'Let me put it this way, Mrs Fisher … may I call you Patricia?' I inclined my head, giving him permission. 'Patricia, I have no illusion that I am anything other than a foolish old man. Forty years ago, if my father had done what I am doing, I would have reacted exactly as Tim has. Actually, if I'm being honest, I doubt I would have been half as tolerant and patient as Tim has been, but I refuse to give up what I have with Betty. It won't last - bright fires burn fast and all that, but while this old man can have one last fling with an attractive woman, I intend to hold onto it with both hands. Figuratively,' he added, just in case I thought he was talking about something else.

'So you believe Betty might be behind the thefts, but you don't want to rock the boat?' I encouraged him to clarify his position.

His unhappy frown returned. 'No, Patricia, that is not what I am saying.' He paced across the room, taking time to work out how to put across what he did want to say. 'I am merely acknowledging that I have been asleep while she was in the cabin, and I have to accept that I cannot state in a court of law that I can account for her movements the whole time she was here.'

'Mr Oswald,' I continued to address him formally since he is a passenger and I was operating as a member of the crew, 'Miss Ross could be guilty of stealing from your son and your granddaughter.'

'Yes, I know!' he snapped, cutting me off with his outburst. 'I'm sorry,' he sighed again. 'Look, I don't think she took anything. Like I said, she has no reason to. If you must know, I have already given her a credit card to use. It's got a ten thousand dollar a day limit on it,' he explained, defending himself because having an insane limit made all the difference.

However, I didn't know about that, and it gave me a new thing to investigate.

'Has she been using it?' I asked.

John's expression changed to one of surprise. 'Oh, I um, I hadn't thought to look. I'll have my accountant check.' He glanced at his watch before adding, 'In a few hours. It's too early on the West Coast right now. I gave her the card to use if she needed to though, I don't care if she has been – it's pocket change.'

Ha! To a billionaire maybe.

'It will give an indication as to whether she is after your money,' I pointed out.

A squeal of shock from another part of the suite was followed by laughter.

Tulisa's voice echoed out, 'Where did you come from?'

I looked around, guiltily realising I had taken my eyes off the dogs. They had gone looking for food more than likely and found their way to wherever Tulisa was.

I started forward, heading for the voice, looking about until I found a door cracked open just wide enough for a dachshund to squeeze through.

When I knocked, the door swung inward a little farther.

'Hello?' I called. 'Is that you, Tulisa? It's Mrs Fisher, the ship's detective. Sorry about the dogs. I didn't realise they had wandered off.'

'That's fine,' she called out, the sound of bare feet on carpet leading to the door swinging fully open as she grabbed it from the inside. 'They are very sweet. Dad won't let me have a dog. He says I wouldn't look after it just because I won't muck out my horses at home. What's the point of having stable hands and a farrier if I am going to do it myself?'

It was valid point. Sort of.

Tulisa had on a pair of slouch shorts that looked like they were part of a pair of short pyjamas. On her top half was a black sheer vest over a bright red bra. She was thin, her frame lean and willowy like a supermodel. There wasn't much curve going on, her frame almost androgynous. I looked away before she could catch me watching her and down at the dogs who were now sniffing around her room.

'Are you coming out of your room today, dear?' John asked, appearing in the doorway behind me. 'Perhaps you could join Betty and me for some dinner. We could clear the air a little.'

She rolled her eyes like only a teenager knows how.

'There is no air to clear, granddad. You're confusing me with dad. Betty and I get on just fine.'

I made a mental note, but there were only a few years between them, so I found the news unsurprising. With no mother and no siblings, Tulisa probably needed someone like Betty to bring her out of her shell. It had to be tough as the granddaughter of a billionaire. Was she set to inherit? Probably, but that had to make friends hard to find.

'Very well,' John was astute enough to avoid getting into an argument with the young woman. 'Will you be good enough to join us then? You can pick the restaurant.'

Not bothering to look at the family patriarch, Tulisa grunted, 'Maybe. I'm not hungry yet.'

'But you haven't eaten today,' John protested, before realising the futility of such an approach. Backing away with his hands up, he said, 'I shall hope that you get hungry later.'

I was turning to follow him, and about to call the dogs to follow me – I needed to quiz John more yet – when I spotted a photograph on the dressing table.

My eyes bulged in time to my jaw hitting the deck. Two quick paces carried me across the room to where I confirmed my eyes were not deceived.

'This is your mother?' I asked, picking up the silver frame to get a better look.

Tulisa came around me to look too.

'Yes. She was so beautiful.'

Tulisa wasn't wrong, her mother was a stunning beauty. I couldn't judge her height from the picture, but I didn't need to. It wasn't really the woman in the picture I was looking at. My need to quiz John or Tulisa about anything had just evaporated and I needed to go.

Sex Work

The moment I was outside the suite, I grabbed my phone from my bag. I was heading for the bridge – I had a sudden, unexpected, and very desperate need to talk to Alistair. I was walking fast, the dogs gamely trotting along in front. Alistair's phone was ringing, and I was clenching my teeth so hard as I waited for him to pick up that my jaw began to hurt.

He didn't answer, the phone switching across to voicemail before I hung up. Not picking up could be for any one of about three dozen reasons, so I pulled out the radio I had in my bag, pressing the send switch and starting to talk before I realised it wasn't working.

The stupid battery was dead because I never check these things.

Muttering to myself, I hurried on, making another phone call, this time to Lieutenant Commander Baker in the operations room.

'Mrs Fisher, you beat me to it,' he said upon answering the phone.

Mystified, I asked, 'Beat you to what?'

'I was just about to call you. We found something in the trash.'

I stopped walking, my feet somehow not able to operate if I needed to listen intently.

'It's a piece of paper with numbers and letters on it. That wouldn't normally mean anything at all, but one of the numbers was two, two, zero, zero and we believe we have figured out what the note means.'

I waited for him to explain, my need to know causing me to prompt him.

'Sorry,' he apologised. 'We are still checking some of the names.'

'Names?' I questioned. 'I thought it was numbers and letters.'

He apologised again. 'Yes. It's a code. It starts with four digits that are a time. Then it's another set of digits to represent the cabin, and it ends with a letter. If you hadn't stolen Mrs Purcell's phone, we never would have figured it out. She is on the list,' he explained. 'It has 22001934P which is ten o'clock in the evening, her cabin, and her initial. We have been cross-referencing the other entries and they all match up to women who are travelling alone. Hold on, Mrs Fisher, I'm switching you to speaker.'

The background tone changed, and Deepa's voice came through the phone.

'We are scrambling some reinforcements to get around the ship as fast as we can. This list reads like a set of targets. Whoever the voice on the phone was, he's going to hit all these women. We have to warn them.'

The back of my head itched, and the alignment of clues had never been more welcome. I laughed when I saw the truth behind the curtain.

The team in the operations room fell silent when they heard me laugh and must have thought I was going bonkers.

'Is everything all right, Mrs Fisher?' Baker asked.

'Yes. You were right about the man planning to 'hit' the ladies on the list, but he's not robbing them. At least, I don't think so. Certainly, that is not his primary intention.'

I had lost them completely. Smiling to myself as I chose to be cruelly cryptic, I said, 'Stand down the reinforcements, please. We won't be needing them. You can meet me in my suite in thirty minutes – I think I have found a way to solve the Oswald case and need to speak with the captain. I will need to make some phone calls, but I believe I will soon have the proof I need to make an arrest. As for the ladies and the codes,

I'll explain when I see you, but we need to tread carefully if we are to catch the man behind it all.'

I started walking away, a little bit of my usual spring returning to my step now that I had a solution to both cases. The stowaway remained an enigma, but I had never held out much hope of solving that case. It was just too mysterious, and the trail of his killer was long cold.

Hurrying through passageways to get to the bridge, I turned a corner and spotted Barbie ahead of me. We locked eyes, just for a second. That was all it took for her expression to change. The perky smile dropped as the corners of her mouth turned down.

She turned away from me, taking a side passage to avoid me as I came her way. What the heck was going on? We were best friends!

'Barbie!' I yelled after her as I started running to catch up. 'Barbie! What's going on? What have I done?'

I got to the passage she had taken and found it empty. The gazelle had bolted, putting in a turn of speed to escape me. I could phone her, but what would be the point in that? I chose to text her instead.

'Barbie, I have no idea what I have done to upset you, but whatever it is, I am truly sorry. Can we talk?' The message left my phone, and I wasted a minute staring at my screen in the hope that she would respond straight away.

When she didn't, I set off again, continuing toward the bridge, but aware the spring had left my step once more. Barbie and I both worked on the same cruise ship – she couldn't avoid me forever. I was going to have it out with her and get to the bottom of what was going on, and I suddenly sensed that I was getting angry. Barbie was making me angry because she was angry. It is an unpleasant emotion, and it is infectious.

I got all the way to the bridge where I found a smartly dressed, young lieutenant manning the door to the elevator. He saw me coming, getting a happy wave from me as I got within talking distance.

'Hello, Pedro, is the captain on the bridge?'

'No, he's behind you.' Alistair joined the list of people who had made me jump today when his voice rang out unexpectedly.

I spun around to find him coming toward me, flanked by the deputy captain, Commander Ochi, and a pair of lieutenants from the security team. Anna and Georgie ran at him, always happy to see someone they knew, and Alistair was a favourite.

Lieutenant Pedro Hannan snapped out a salute behind me – I could tell because Alistair returned it before bending to meet the dogs. They got a pat each which was sufficient to placate them.

'You were looking for me?' Alistair asked.

Commander Ochi gave me a nod as he passed, heading up to the bridge and not waiting for the captain. The security guards moved to one side, remaining behind to mind their principle.

'Yes,' I moved in close because what I needed to say was sensitive. 'I need to see the receipt for the necklace you bought me.'

I didn't explain any further so of course Alistair frowned with doubtful misunderstanding.

'That is not something I feel a desire to show you, my love. Why do you need to see it?'

I pulled a face that I hoped would show how difficult this was for me.

'You don't have to show me the figure at the bottom of it; that's your business. I just need to see the name of the jeweller and I need his phone number.'

Alistair's frown deepened. 'Whatever for, darling? Is there something wrong with it?'

Oh, Lord. How do I explain this? I caught his elbow with my right hand and tugged him away from the two lieutenants who were definitely within earshot. They were trying to look like they were not listening, but I wasn't willing to risk it.

'It's stolen,' I whispered. 'It is one of the stolen items I am investigating. I just saw a picture of Tim Oswald's dead wife and she was wearing it around her neck. There is no way it is not the same piece.' Alistair's face was incredulous. I pressed on. 'Remember when we saw it, the jeweller was just putting it in the window. I figured he had been cleaning it or something, but I think he had just bought it from someone who came into the shop before we got there, someone from the ship.'

'Miss Ross?' Alistair sought to confirm, once again showing off how much he knew about everything going on around him.

'Yes, that would be my guess, but I noticed the CCTV cameras in the shop when we were in there.'

'Of course you did,' commented Alistair dryly.

I dismissed any thought of responding, Alistair was disappointed to hear about the necklace, of course. 'If he has footage of the person who brought in the necklace, then ...'

'You can wrap up the case rather neatly,' Alistair completed my sentence. He nodded his head, stiffly because he was making deliberate motions to stop himself from responding emotionally. 'You should come up to my quarters, I have the receipt there.'

There was no need to say anything further. Lieutenant Hannan opened the elevator which carried us into the superstructure that rose high above the rest of the ship. A few minutes later, Alistair returned to where I was waiting – he obviously wanted to keep what he spent a secret, and I wasn't going to invade his privacy even though I was really rather curious.

I used my phone to take a picture of the details on the bottom of the receipt. He had folded it and was holding it in such a way that the figure wasn't visible.

A young lieutenant walked by, saluting as she went, and when Alistair returned it, he had to shift the hand in which he had the receipt and I saw the eye-watering number even though I promised myself I would never look.

When he looked back in my direction, I was doing my best to make my face look normal.

'Everything all right, dear?' he asked, eyeing me curiously.

I touched a hand to my belly. 'My stomach is a little off,' I bluffed, hoping that would explain my odd expression. I held up my phone. 'I have what I need. This should close the case, as you said. I'll let you know how it goes. Oh,' I added. 'I think I have figured out the other one as well.'

'The stowaway?' he questioned.

'No, the other, other one. Mrs Evelyn Goodwin, the one who was posed after she died. I think I know who posed her and why, I just need to prove it, but again … I'll let you know when I have a definite result.'

Alistair accepted my reluctance to tell him any more than that, checking over his shoulder before stealing a kiss.

'Do you believe you will be finished in time to join me tonight?' The question was laced with suggestion; the hunger in his eyes for something other than food. It caused a ripple of excitement in my core.

'I certainly hope to be,' I murmured, my voice little more than a whisper.

We kissed again, just a peck, and then the elevator doors swished open, a fresh set of officers exiting the car with salutes when they spotted their captain right outside.

I stepped into the silver box, Alistair refusing to take his eyes off me until the doors closed to form a barrier between us. A sigh escaped my lips – I was punching above my weight dating the captain of the ship. He was not only inexcusably handsome, he also had power and respect, and he had money. Okay, so I have my own money, and finding a man to support me would never enter my head, but he was financially stable and that was an attractive quality in a man. He was sensible, unlike my ex-husband, Charlie, but more importantly, he was caring, and tender, and emotionally available.

It was hard not to scream about how much in love with him I was. Were it not for the fact that I was still waiting for the finalised divorce paperwork to come through, I would be imagining diamond rings and humming the wedding march. As it was, I couldn't entertain the idea of getting married again.

Not yet.

The elevator arrived at the top deck, spitting me out and bursting the bubble of daydream I had slipped into.

I was heading for my suite where I expected to find Baker and the rest of the team converging shortly – I was ready to reveal my genius. Would Barbie be there? Thinking about my suite reminded me of the situation with my roomie. She was most likely with Hideki though – he'd said they were getting together tonight.

Maybe she would be in a better mood and ready to talk in the morning.

Checking my watch, I still had enough minutes left to make the call to the jeweller so I did precisely that, praying it would connect.

'Good afternoon, Arthur English, fine jewellery for discerning customers,' the jeweller rattled off his practised spiel. 'How might I help you today?'

I needed to balance this right. If I told the man he was peddling stolen goods, I worried he might just hang up the phone. Nevertheless, I was going to have to broach the subject.

'Hello, this is Patricia Fisher, I was in your shop yesterday. My boyfriend bought me the five-carat sapphire necklace.'

'Oh, yes!' he gushed. 'An exquisite piece. Are you looking for some matching earrings? I have just the item in the shop. I could easily adjust the setting to exactly match the necklace.'

I kept my tone engaging. 'Not just yet, thank you though. Perhaps when we come back around. I was hoping you might be able to tell me something about the person who sold you the necklace. You had recently purchased it when we came in, hadn't you?'

'Why, yes,' Arthur replied, his tone turning curious.

It took me a while, carefully dancing around the subject, but I steered him to question for himself whether he might have been handling stolen goods. He was clearly mortified by the idea or doing a great job of acting so.

Either way, he promised to review the CCTV footage and email some stills over to me. He could not apologise enough, but truly I thought he was more concerned about repercussions than he was about losing money.

The phone call carried me all the way back to my suite where I could hear voices inside as I pushed the door open.

Jermaine appeared a heartbeat later, taking the dog leads from my hand as I came into the suite's living area.

'Good afternoon, madam,' he greeted me. 'I am led to believe that there have been some developments in the cases you are currently investigating.'

Arranged round my couches, all sipping on freshly prepared coffee, though they had all risen to their feet when I came in as if I were royalty, were the five security officers in their white uniforms.

'Mrs Fisher,' Lieutenant Commander Baker addressed me for the group.

I waved for them to sit again. 'Please, chaps, and you, Deepa, there's no need to stand when I come into the room. What is that all about?' I carried on talking so none of them could answer. 'You want to know what is going on with the coded numbers and the Italian man at the end of the phone, yes?'

'I found the piece of paper with the codes on,' Sam flashed his goofy grin proudly.

'He did,' Lieutenant Commander Baker reached across to clap my assistant on the shoulder. 'Sam was thoroughly diligent.'

'We have decided the man on the phone is Italian then?' Schneider asked.

I looked at him since he had spoken. 'Yes, It's Ricardo Rossini. He's a gigolo.' I let my statement sink in and got to watch Lieutenant Pippin do a fist pump to congratulate himself.

'Who's Ricardo Rossini?' asked Sam.

'Pippin found him,' I revealed, giving credit where it was due. 'Without his dedicated efforts, I wouldn't know who we were after.' I went on to explain how Pippin had found the handsome, middle-aged Italian man by studying the cameras high above the restaurants. 'Evelyn took out a wad of cash which went missing without a trace. That's because she gave it to Ricardo. He didn't steal it; she was paying him for a service. It's also the reason why her sister, Priscilla, refused to speak to us about the subject. She knew who had been in her sister's cabin, maybe she did help to pose Evelyn, but I think we can rule out murder and theft.'

'She had a heart attack in the throes of passion,' Deepa murmured.

Baker said, 'What a way to go,' his words echoing everyone's thoughts.

'Wait a second though.' Pippin raised his hand like he was in school and dropped it again when everyone looked at him. 'If he is ... servicing,' he picked the word carefully, 'these ladies, doesn't that conflict with him being gay. He is travelling with his husband.'

It was a valid point and one I had considered.

Jermaine coughed politely, drawing attention his way.

'If Mrs Fisher's assumptions are correct, and they have a tendency of being so, then Ricardo Rossini is not gay, he is bisexual.'

I had to wonder how his relationship with his husband worked if he was out all night 'servicing' the needs of lonely older women and a thought occurred to me.

'Remember when we followed Priscilla to the coffee shop?'

'How could we forget it?' asked Deepa, bringing a tinge of red to my cheeks.

Pressing on to cover my embarrassment, I said, 'She was meeting other ladies. They were all the right age and none of them seemed to be travelling with a husband.'

Baker nodded. 'We already recognised a few of them when we cross-referenced their cabin numbers against the initial on the codes.'

'How many were there?' I enquired, curious to hear how many cabins Ricardo was able to get through in a night.

'Six,' replied Deepa. 'Starting at eight o'clock, but not all of them had a full hour slot, there were two with half hour sessions.

'If we assume it's five hundred dollars an hour, that's a decent pile of money. How long had Ricardo Rossini been on the ship?' I asked the team, certain they would know.

'Since Rome,' supplied Baker. It was almost two weeks. 'They are staying on until the ship returns to Italy in three months' time,' He added.

'Except they won't be, surely?' Jermaine enquired. 'They might not have committed a crime ...'

'But sex work is not something Purple Star will tolerate,' I completed what he was thinking. 'No, we are going to catch him in the act, and he will be ejected at the next port.'

'Can't we just have some of his ... clients,' once again Pippin had to search for an appropriate and polite term to employ, 'admit the truth? With statements from them, we won't need to do anything else,' he pointed out.

He was absolutely right, but Baker saw the trouble with his plan.

'The ladies involved do not want us to take away their entertainment. They will know the likely result of revealing the truth and will deny everything. If we approach them, it is more likely that they will tip off Ricardo and then we lose the chance to catch him.'

Deepa cottoned on to what I was suggesting, her eyes widening when she stared right at me.

'You're going to reverse honeytrap them, aren't you?' she blurted.

'I'm a little young compared to their usual clientele, but I disguised myself once today. I'm sure adding a few years will not prove too difficult.' The memory of my latest wrinkle resurfaced. 'I make myself available and record him propositioning me.'

'That actually sounds quite easy,' commented Schneider, picturing the bust in his head. 'Once we have him in custody, the ladies might be more inclined to tell the truth.'

'And we can put him under the spotlight to confirm what really happened to Evelyn Goodwin.' I concluded.

I stopped speaking at the same moment my phone began ringing. Right on cue, Arthur English was calling me, and it had to be with good news. With my fingers crossed, I thumbed the green button to connect the call.

'What do you have for me, Mr English?'

'Mrs Fisher,' his voice rang in my ear. 'I have sent a file to the email address you supplied. Do you have it?'

'One moment.' I excused myself to switch between apps on my phone. I doubted I would be able to see the pictures very well on the tiny screen, but dropping into my emails, I was able to confirm his message was there. I thanked him and said we would come back to him if we had any further questions.

The phone conversation had been private, so the team was now watching me to hear what the call had been about. With their eyes on me, I pointed across the room to the desk and the tower computer set up there.

'I have something to show you all. I think this will be of interest.'

When I wove across the room to get to the desk, they left their positions on the couches to follow me. I didn't make them wait long. I also didn't explain what we were looking at until the pictures were on the screen.

'This is a jewellery store in Gibraltar, where a necklace that belonged to Tim Oswald's deceased wife was sold.'

'That's Betty Ross,' stated Baker, clearly surprised that she had lied – I hadn't gotten around to telling the team what I learned from Betty's mother.

The picture was a little fuzzy, and shot facing the counter inside, the still was of Miss Ross when she was turning to leave, and her motion added to the blurriness. The ample chest, hidden by a halter top that came up around her neck, and a three-quarter length pink leather jacket that covered her shoulders, was still there to be seen. Her shock of blonde hair hid a chunk of her face, but it was her all right, and I was willing to bet we would find the clothes we could see her wearing hanging in the closet in her cabin.

'Shall we go?' I asked.

Mystery Redhead

Betty had lied about it all. She was sleeping with John Oswald for his money, and it made me mad. He was a sweet old man who had been duped by a woman with loose morals and a criminal mind. It didn't matter that he had billions and ought to know better, she had targeted him much the same as a mugger went after the unsuspecting.

The time it took to get to her cabin did nothing to quash my ire. Honestly, I felt like having Schneider kick her door off its hinges.

There was no need for that though, one swipe on the door's keypad with a universal key card and we were in. There was no quarrel from the team this time; we had full justification for entering her cabin, though I gave Baker the chance to knock once.

When Betty didn't answer, I wondered if we would need to go looking for her, but she was in her cabin, appearing suddenly and looking shocked at our intrusion. She hadn't answered when Lieutenant Commander Baker knocked and called out and I guessed that was to give her a chance to hide whatever stolen things she still had in her cabin.

'Miss Ross you are under arrest,' I declared, sweeping into the cabin with the security team both ahead and behind me. 'I found the jewellers where you sold the sapphire necklace,' I met her shocked face with a wolf's leer. 'It was all just for money, wasn't it? How much did you manage to squirrel away? We will be taking it all back.'

The team had fanned out, Schneider and Bhukari blocking the door while Sam and Pippin were waiting for Baker's orders.

'Will you make us search the cabin?' Baker asked. 'Or will you be good enough to tell us where you just stashed the Oswalds' belongings?'

Betty finally overcame her shock to say, 'I have no idea what you are talking about. I haven't stolen anything! Why won't you people believe me?' she repeated the same lines she'd been employing all day. 'And I certainly didn't sell anything to a jeweller in Gibraltar,' she added. 'Whatever would make you think that I did?'

'Photographic evidence,' I replied, as matter-of-factly as I could. 'You were picked up by the CCTV camera in the shop.'

To prove my point and end her argument, I held up my phone so she could see the damning picture of her as she turned to leave Mr English's shop.

Her eyes bugged out, much as I expected they would.

'That's not me,' she protested.

Baker clicked his fingers. 'Chaps please inspect Miss Ross's wardrobe for a three-quarter length blush pink leather jacket and a white halter neck top.'

'Hey!' Betty Ross's brow creased in anger as Sam and Pippin opened her closet and started rifling through her clothes. It was invasive, but that is what you get when you decide to start robbing people.

She was wise enough to stay where she was, her frustration and embarrassment hiking up another notch when Sam pulled out the pink leather jacket.

'Is this it?' he questioned.

They had drawn a blank on the white halter neck top but that changed when Pippin found the drawer with her dirty laundry.

She complained again, but how could she fight the evidence now? Despite what I thought, she tried anyway.

'Look, I'm telling you, that isn't me. I didn't venture into Gibraltar. I only got off to take some selfies and poke around. I certainly didn't go into a jewellery store, so, you need to keep looking for whoever that is.'

Tired of hearing her lies, I nodded to Lieutenant's Schneider and Bhukari who came silently past me to take Miss Ross into custody. She was weeping, the effect of being caught causing an emotional reaction.

'Will you tell us where the rest of the jewellery and cash is stashed?' I asked.

She spat something unprintable in reply and was gone, on her way to the brig where she would be held while we constructed her case.

Once she was gone, her sobbing denials of any wrongdoing fading into the distance, Baker said, 'We've got this, Mrs Fisher. There's no need for you to stay. Are you going to track down Ricardo Rossini now? We need to deal with this, but I can drum up some support in just a few minutes.'

I gave Lieutenant Commander Baker a tired smile.

'I'm going to have some lunch and a rest.' It was well after noon – closer to dinner time than it was lunch for that matter, but it wasn't unusual for me to get lost in what I was doing. 'I think we will be best placed to catch Mr Rossini later today. When Bhukari and Schneider have dealt with Miss Ross and found the time to eat, if they have not already, then they can locate Mr Rossini and we can go from there.'

I was telling myself it was too early in the day for the Italian to be out delivering his 'goods'. I suspected I could be entirely wrong, but since he almost certainly wasn't endangering anyone – what happened to Evelyn notwithstanding – I figured he could wait a while.

Back at my suite, I patted the dachshunds and let Jermaine make me a pot of tea. I slumped on the longest couch, kicking my shoes off and swinging my legs up to tuck them under myself. The dachshunds arrived on top of me before I could even get comfortable, the promise of ear scratches and a warm lap too much to pass up.

Jermaine made me smoked salmon and cucumber sandwiches, delivering them on a side table within easy reach while I decompressed my brain by watching a little television.

When he came to collect the empty cup, saucer, and plate, I turned my attention away from the flat screen on the opposite wall to ask him a question.

'Do you know what is troubling Barbie? I know I asked you already, but that was when I thought she might have something bothering her. Now, given her behaviour toward me, it's clear she is upset with me about something, and I don't know what it could be.'

Jermaine's face remained locked in butler mode – no emotion displayed whatsoever. Unfortunately for him, I know that means he is carefully not saying what it is that he has to say.

'Jermaine,' I growled. 'If you know what is going on, you have to tell me. I have no idea how I have managed to upset her, and I need to find out so I can make it right.'

Balancing the tray with the cutlery and crockery on his left hand, he folded his right hand behind his back.

'Miss Berkeley reacted to the content of an email you sent her, madam,' he revealed. 'I do not feel it would be proper for me to say any more than that.'

'An email,' I echoed his words, dredging my brain to come up with when I last sent Barbie an email. Had I ever sent her one?

Confused, I picked up my phone, opened the email app and started scrolling down through the entries. There were no emails to Barbie in the last two weeks – the maximum period the phone held – but I'd known that without needing to look.

Barbie had been fine with me yesterday, and then ... poof! Getting ever more irked by the silly situation we found ourselves in, I chose to message her. I couldn't betray Jermaine's trust and reveal he had spoken to me, but equally, I refused to just leave things as they were.

'Barbie, I know you are upset with me and don't wish to discuss the matter, yet I believe you have been tricked somehow. We were fine yesterday, and I have not said anything to you or sent you any messages since then that could warrant your desire to distance yourself from me. We need to talk. Something is going on.' The message whizzed out of my phone and into the ether, winging its way to Barbie's phone where I felt certain she would read it.

I was just about to put my phone down again when it pinged, the sound of an incoming email chiming in the quiet of my suite.

The email was from Barbie. Or so I thought. Well, what I mean to say is that it was sent by Barbie but her email contained only another email, one sent to her by me.

Except it wasn't.

Confused yet? I know I am. I was reading an email that had come from my email address and was written using words I might employ.

Barbie,

Now that I have a team of dedicated security agents to aid me with my investigations, I feel you ought to take a back seat. Really, I'm surprised I have to point this out to you, for it should have been obvious that your continued interference in my cases is becoming embarrassing to the real detectives.

I value our friendship and hope this will not mar our relationship.

Yours

Patricia

If there is a better term to use than jaw-on-the-floor, then I don't know what it is. Obviously, I hadn't written a word of the email and the thoughts expressed in it had never entered my head. Barbie was as much a part of my ability to solve cases as anyone else. She had been instrumental in taking down the Godmother and were it not for her help when I first came on board, I might still be rotting in a jail in St Kitts, awaiting a trial for murder.

I tried phoning her, but she still didn't want to pick up. I guess I couldn't blame her now, but two questions surfaced. The first was to do with how I was going to prove to Barbie that I hadn't sent the email, but the second one was just as important – who did?

Someone was messing with me, and they were doing it deliberately. Whoever it was had gotten hold of my phone or snuck into my suite to log in and pretend to be me. It sort of explained the complaints too since they were all fabrications.

I was going to track her down and make her listen, but I sent her a quick text message anyway.

'I did not send that email! I need your help to find out who did. How could you think I sent those awful words?'

Okay, so it was a little cruel to spin it back onto her, but I genuinely wanted to ask how she could think I would write something so despicably vile and hurtful.

From the kitchen, I heard the sound of a radio squawking into life.

'Jermaine, it's Deepa, is Mrs Fisher there?'

My eyebrows knitted as I looked across to find Jermaine lifting the radio to his mouth.

'Yes, Lieutenant Bhukari. Mrs Fisher is here.'

I carefully angled my lap so the dogs slid onto the couch cushions before I got up to see what was happening now.

'Why have you got a radio?' I asked guiltily remembering the one in my handbag with its dead battery.

Jermaine, his face doing its best to remain emotionless, said, 'Lieutenant Commander Baker expressed a concern that your radio keeps going missing, or running out of battery or ... befalls an unfortunate accident that renders it useless for future use. He believed supplying me with one might be an expedient solution to their occasional trouble locating you.'

I frowned at him, my eyebrows doing all the talking. It didn't matter that they were right; they were ganging up on me because I was rubbish with the radios.

'Mrs Fisher?' Deepa's voice carried over the airwaves. 'We have a problem in the detention centre. Can you come down, please?'

Jermaine handed me the radio.

I pressed the send button and started talking.

'I'm on my way. What's going on?'

The dogs were trying to follow me, but I didn't want to take them down into the bowels of the ship where the brig was located well away from anywhere a passenger might accidentally roam. Jermaine intercepted them, scooping them to his chest, one under each arm where they wagged their tails at me and sniffed the air coming from outside when I opened the door again.

'I won't be long. I hope,' I added, just in case it was hours before I returned. Deepa had been talking the whole time as I grabbed my handbag and slipped on my shoes, so I knew what I would be facing when I got down to the brig.

Unfortunately, on a ship the size of the Aurelia, getting places can take a while. It's basically a floating town set over twenty decks. The passengers have access to the top fourteen decks with the lower six, most of which were below the water line, reserved for crew accommodation, storage rooms, the giant engines, and whatever else they could cram in. The ship has to carry fresh water and have a water recycling plant because the thousands of passengers on board all want to take a shower or a bath every day. Then there is laundry and cooking and that's just some of the things the ship needs water for.

I got to the brig twenty minutes after leaving my suite, but by then it was all over. I met Betty Ross on her way out.

'I told you I didn't steal anything and that I didn't go into a jewellery store in Gibraltar,' she spat at me.

Keeping my tone even, I replied, 'But you did not say that you had an alibi for the time we believed you were ashore.'

'She didn't want to involve me,' said John Oswald. He was standing directly behind her and had provided the alibi that dictated her release. Lieutenants Bhukari and Schneider had hopped to it, checking out his claim to be certain he wasn't lying to clear her name, but he was telling the truth.

John Oswald was a well-travelled man and had no interest in visiting Gibraltar. In his words, it was a dumb piece of rock with some tunnels and too many monkeys. Instead, he had booked a couple's massage for himself and Betty and the two of them were in the company of crew members when I believed Miss Ross was ashore selling the necklace.

I was blocking their exit quite deliberately. I could swallow my pride and admit I had it wrong. And though I wanted to, I would not point out again that Miss Ross could have avoided her brief incarceration by being more forthcoming.

Turning my attention to her lover, I said, 'Someone took that necklace out of your son's bedroom, Mr Oswald. Whoever it is, they also broke into Betty's cabin and took her clothes for fear they might be spotted. Someone tried to set you up,' I pointed out. 'You must have some idea who it is? Did you say all your friends left the ship already? Is there someone else on board who might want to hurt your reputation?'

'No,' Betty groaned. 'I have no idea who could be behind it, but what if they are not trying to hurt me at all.'

‘That’s right,’ John agreed. ‘We were just talking about this, trying to work out who could be behind it. Maybe it’s someone who needs money and spotted Betty in my company. They could be committing an opportunistic crime and posing as Betty to hide their true identity.’

‘I bought my pink jacket on the ship,’ Betty pointed out, not doing anything to hide the irritation in her voice. ‘Anyone else could have bought one.’

The concept that someone had deliberately chosen to pose as Betty was improbable to the point that it sounded like something from a really garbage spy movie. I couldn’t argue though. Not yet. But keeping quiet about it was okay because I planned to figure out who her accomplice was. Then I was going to arrest her again and it would stick next time.

Lieutenants Schneider and Bhukari exited the main room of the detention centre to join us in the passageway that led to the door to get out.

‘That’s all the paperwork done,’ said Schneider. ‘We can escort you back to the passenger decks if you are ready?’ He raised his eyebrows in question, swivelling his gaze to check with them and with me.

‘I have nothing further,’ I offered. ‘I’m sorry that you had to go through the arrest, but now we can be sure someone has chosen to pose as you, catching them should be easier.’

‘Why is that?’ asked Betty.

‘Because now we know it isn’t you. Up until now you were not only the primary suspect, you were the only one. I would have happily considered someone else but there was no one else to point the finger at.’

My skull itched, a sure sign I was onto something. I fell silent, consulting my brain and begging it to reveal what it had just figured out. It wouldn't come, and my thoughts were interrupted by Mr Oswald Senior speaking.

'Is there something we are waiting for?' he wanted to know.

I was still blocking their exit, taking a pause to think which delayed their departure for even longer and for no good reason. Snapping back to reality, I apologised and moved out of the way.

Schneider called the guards in the detention centre to open the main door and they filed out, the tall Austrian leading the way back to the elevator and escape. I drifted along behind, still lost in my thoughts.

Electing to wait for the next elevator, I focused on trying to figure out who was behind the thefts. Someone was, but they were hiding in the shadows, out of sight. For now.

The sun was down by the time I made it back up to the passenger decks and above the waterline. The sun setting generally meant the outside portions of the ship cleared - fewer passengers wanted to be outside in the cooler air and of course the pools were less appealing once the sun had gone to bed.

Ricardo Rossini would be out to stalk his next victim, or he soon would be, the handsome Italian charming his way into the cabin of passenger after passenger and giving them an experience that was not on the Purple Star Lines list of on-board activities.

It was time to alter my appearance, ageing my face and hair and changing my clothes for something that would hide my arms and legs because even though I had aged – the wrinkle reminded me - my skin betrayed I was a way off from my seventies.

I stopped by the upper deck spa where John and Betty had their couple's massage, just to check for myself.

Wanda, a Russian woman in her forties who was five feet five inches tall and had to weigh about ninety pounds, confirmed the treatment had been booked under John's name and told me the massages had been conducted by Olga and Sergei. They were off duty now and the spa was due to close in a few minutes. If I wanted to speak to them, I was going to have to wait until the morning or track them down below decks.

I thanked Wanda and continued to drift through the ship, my mind elsewhere until my way was suddenly blocked by a tall woman.

I hadn't been paying attention and thought I had gotten in her way.

However, when I said, 'I'm sorry, please excuse me,' and attempted to go around her, she moved to block my path again.

This time I looked up at her face. She was six foot in her heels and slender like a person who works out a lot and eats sensibly. In her forties, she had flaming natural red hair that cascaded from her skull in a sensual flow over one shoulder.

The word to describe her was statuesque.

Fiery green eyes looked down at me.

'Hmmm,' she made a noise with her mouth before she spoke. 'I expected something more. He said you were pretty. He didn't say you were old and a bit baggy around the middle. I wonder what he was thinking.' Her accent was elegant, and European, making me think she might be Swiss and seriously rich.

Taken aback, it was clear she was talking about Alistair, but I had no idea who she was. I opened my mouth to speak, intending to demand to know her name and what she was talking about, but she cut me off before I could make a sound.

'I'm taking him back,' she replied. 'Or rather, I already have. You should show some self-respect and just accept that you were never good enough for him. Crying and getting upset won't change anything, but it will embarrass you.'

'Who are you?' I growled, the dramas of the last day or so fuelling my rising ire.

She stepped into my personal space, looming over me as she poked a long, manicured fingernail into my collar bone – jab, jab, jab.

'I'm the one who is going to kick your butt if you don't back off and leave him alone. Alistair Huntley is mine, understand?'

I took a step back, adrenaline demanding I get ready to fight or run. It was true that quite a few people had threatened to hurt or kill me in the last few months, but this was up close and personal, and it was happening right now.

Doing my best to be brave, I said, 'I understand that Alistair loves me. I understand *that*, you delusional madwoman.'

She took another step toward me, making me squeal and duck away as she tried to grab me. Voices echoing along the passageway reached our ears, the crazy redhead abandoning her lunge but jabbing a finger in my direction again.

'Be warned, tiny, old woman. Alistair is mine and you will know it soon enough.'

She turned and walked away just as some passengers appeared behind me. I was too shocked to think to call for security or I might have had them apprehend her.

Just in case I didn't have enough going on, now I had a mad woman trying to convince me to break up with Alistair so that she could have a go.

I was going to have to ask Alistair about it because, of course, he wasn't sleeping with her or anything. The idea of it made me sick and I had to lower my head to stop it spinning. Could I take another man cheating on me the way my husband had?

The answer was a firm no, and I told myself I was just being silly. The redhead, whoever she was, had a screw loose. That was all. Nothing more.

How wrong was I?

Old Patricia

I came into my suite to find Barbie resting on a couch with her legs crossed in the lotus position. A magazine was spread across her lap, her attention on it, but she heard me coming through the door and looked at me with a concerned face.

Only for a second though. She unfolded her legs in a single sinuous move and stood up, putting the dogs, who were hidden by the magazine, and the magazine itself to one side.

The dogs stretched and yawned on the couch behind as she walked across the room. Getting closer, she unfolded her arms, which had been crossed in front of her chest, and pulled me into a hug.

'I checked your email account. I hope that's okay,' she murmured, her face buried in my hair as she held me and refused to let go. 'The email didn't come from you, and you know what that means?' she asked.

No, I genuinely didn't.

Pushing back to get some space, she chuckled at me. 'Patty you are so funny. It means someone has cloned your email account. They did a good job too. Usually, emails someone created in a cloned account appear in the user's email chain, but the person behind this must have some sophisticated software because there's no sign of who did it.'

'Can we catch them?' I asked, imagining it would be the same person who was behind the string of complaints.

Barbie shrugged which was scary because she is such a whizz with all the IT stuff.

What she said was, 'It won't be easy. Do you forgive me for getting upset?'

I couldn't believe she felt a need to ask. 'Of course, Barbie. You're my bestie. Just, next time come and speak to me, okay?'

She nodded her head and we hugged again. At least one thing was back to normal, but as I thought that, an idea occurred to me.

'I think you should move out,' I blurted before my brain caught up with my mouth.

Barbie looked like I had just slapped her.

'What? Why?'

'Because whoever is behind this is trying to mess with my life,' I thought about the complaints, and then about the psycho redhead and questioned if she was yet another part of that same plot. Was she the one behind it all?

I gasped, startling Barbie who begged to know if I was okay.

I told her about the statuesque redhead and what she said in the quiet passageway, and I told her about the false complaints people had been sending to Purple Star HQ.

'It's a whole hate campaign,' Barbie murmured. 'Do you think it could be the Godmother reaching out from jail?'

To be honest, the thought had yet to occur to me, but now Barbie had said it, a chill ran down my spine. We had destroyed the Godmother's organisation, stripping it down to almost nothing, but there had to be players left in the field that were yet to be caught or were not on the database of information we revealed to the world. That one of them might be on board and targeting me was terrifying. It was also worryingly easy to believe.

I shook my head though. 'No, it feels too subtle for her. She might send an assassin, but hacking my emails to force us apart lacks punch. It could be the redhead though.'

Barbie started toward the desk and the computer.

'We need to trawl through pictures until we find her.' She was suggesting we access central registry and use it to find out who she was.

'No time,' I argued. 'I need your help to make me look old. Can you call someone from one of the costume departments?'

The ship had more than twelve theatres, each putting on a different kind of show. Barbie had called upon them before when we needed disguises and tonight was going to be no different.

While Barbie sent messages to see who was available to help, I took the radio from my handbag.

Yay! It had some battery left in it! Ha! Strike one up for the middle-aged woman.

I got Deepa and Schneider on the channel reserved for security use and got them on the hunt for Ricardo Rossini. They would circulate his picture to all the crew via their tablets and he would be located soon enough unless he was in a cabin, um ... getting busy.

It was only six o'clock and I was willing to bet he was yet to venture out.

Waiting for word from my team, and for Barbie's theatre people to arrive, Barbie invited me over to the computer to play a clever version of the old guess who game.

‘I think the computer can do this,’ she commented as she opened the passenger central registry. ‘Right. Redhead,’ she was talking to herself as she input details into the search bar.

The computer sifted the results, narrowing down thousands of passengers to just a few hundred.

‘You said she was in her forties?’

I nodded. ‘Yes. Early forties. Like ten years younger than me, or maybe a little more.’

Barbie put that in, and the list reduced to less than fifty. Fifty was a manageable number. It was going to have to wait though because simultaneously, there came a knock at the door and the radio squawked – Schneider calling Deepa, Sam, Pippin and their boss, Lieutenant Commander Baker to his location. He had spotted both Mr Rossinis leaving their cabin. He was tailing them at a safe distance but needed cover in case they spotted him.

Baker and Pippin were still in their uniforms, Sam too, but Deepa and Schneider were in their civilian clothes, acting as passengers to get close to Ricardo without tipping him off.

The dogs had exploded in their usual cacophony of barking as they shot across the room to sniff at the gap under the door and wag their tails while waiting to find out who was outside.

Barbie followed them, calling out to Jermaine who was coming from his adjoining cabin. I knew him well enough to know he was in there to give Barbie and me the space we needed.

‘There’s someone at the door, sweetie,’ she smiled at him teasingly as she got closer to the door. Don’t rush, I’ll get it.’

'Don't you dare,' he warned her, walking slowly across the suite in a deliberately unhurried manner. Barbie wasn't really going to answer the door. She would tease her friend regularly, but would never deliberately undermine him in his duties.

Jermaine opened the door, two ladies ploughing through it with bundles of clothes in their arms and a small suitcase trailing behind them.

'We are short on time,' the first announced.

Jermaine hurried to announce them.

'Madam, I have the honour to name Miss Madrigal Mayhem ...'

'It's her stage name,' Barbie whispered in my ear. 'She does a cabaret act with magic.'

'And Miss Sixpence Tuppence,' Jermaine introduced the second lady, trundling in after the first.

'Wow, that's a cool stage name,' I waved hello to the second woman.

Barbie flared her eyes at me and gave an almost imperceptible shake of her head.

'It's my real name,' replied Sixpence, a little snark making its way into her reply.

I made an 'oops' face, but Madrigal was all about getting the job done so she could get back in time to prepare for her act.

I did as instructed, stripping down to my undies once Jermaine left the room and played the part of a life-sized dolly for the women to dress up. They used makeup to age my face, that was the easy part, they said. Hiding my arms and legs was the hard bit.

Only it wasn't in the end because my legs were covered in a thick pair of flesh-toned tights, complete with ladders in them. They even pulled them down a little so they gathered on my shins to make my legs look shrivelled. That was all very good, but we were off the coast of Africa, and it wasn't exactly cold. I had air conditioning in my suite, but the moment I went outside, I was going to melt, and the tights came up to just under my boobs.

To clad the rest of me was the least flattering dress I had ever worn. It looked to have been hewn from a pair of curtains my grandmother used to have – a hotchpotch of greens and yellows all fighting each other as if a hippo ate grass and bananas until it was sick.

On their instruction, I took off my bra, they wanted my chest to be flat and shapeless which at fifty-three was exactly what they got. They still argued that it had too much volume for a woman in her seventies, so they strapped it all down with some handy bandages. They had a grey wig for my hair and a set of fake teeth to cover my top row which they said were too perfect. The fakes were the weirdest thing I had ever had in my mouth.

Blocky, awful shoes went on my feet. They were at least a size too small and painful to walk in, but I wasn't planning to have them on for long.

Standing back to admire their handiwork, Madrigal and Sixpence nodded their heads in unison – they were happy with the end result and performed a high five without needing to look at each other. There was a floor to ceiling mirror by the door, which when I crossed to it had someone else's reflection looking back at me.

Staring at myself with disbelieving eyes, I said, 'Now I don't need to imagine what I will look like in twenty-five years.'

'Ha!' snorted Barbie. 'There's no way you'll survive another twenty-five years, Patty. Not with your record.' She was joking but I couldn't help but feel the seeds of doubt creeping into my soul. Was I going to run out of luck one day? Would one of my cases go wrong?

I had to admit that it wasn't beyond the realm of possibility. I had been kidnapped, shot at, nearly blown up, and each of those had happened more than once. I couldn't begin to count the number of times I'd needed to run away in order to stay alive.

Before I could question my choices and change my mind about this latest escapade, Barbie hooked a hand through my arm and tugged me toward the door.

'Come on, Patty. Let's go catch a gigolo.'

False Teeth

My team had done the hard part of finding Ricardo. I spoke with them using the radio – check me out. I not only had one with some battery life in it, I even remembered to pick it up and then used it.

I meant to say, 'It's Patricia, where are you?' but my fake teeth ejected themselves from my mouth on the P of Patricia and I had to lunge to catch them with my free hand.

Baker was the first to respond. 'Say again, over.'

Now holding my teeth in my right hand, with Barbie cackling like a child next to me, I tried the radio again.

'It's Patricia,' I repeated, having no trouble this time because the teeth were in my hand. 'Where are you and where is Ricardo?'

They were in the Tiki Bar on deck seventeen. It sat right in the middle of the ship on the port side with great views out over the ocean through floor to ceiling panoramic windows. It even had a terrace outside where passengers could enjoy cocktails in the warm air.

As expected, the warm air was a problem, and I was sweating like a pig by the time I got to the bar. I couldn't breathe either, the bandages around my chest choosing to tighten themselves somehow. It was how I imagined being squeezed by a boa constrictor might feel. Add to that the teeth which were threatening to rebel on every hard consonant, the too-tight shoes, and the wig which was making my head sweat and itch like mad, I was not having a good time.

'We need to wrap this up fast,' I spoke into the radio for the team to hear. I had to enunciate my words carefully, taking time to think about what my lips were going to do so I could control my teeth.

My plan was a really simple one. I was going to sit next to him, start chatting, and lament about my long-dead husband. Then I would slip into the conversation that I was terribly lonely and leave the path wide open for him to strike.

The moment he accepted money from me, he was done.

Pippin met us outside, swapping my radio, a small one but still far too clunky and obvious for me to use in the bar. He had an earpiece that would pick up my voice and allow me to hear everyone else.

'Where's Mrs Fisher?' he asked Barbie, looking around and ignoring me.

I raised my hand and waved. 'Right here, Pippin,' I spat my teeth at him on the first P of Pippin and swore as I had to lunge to catch them again.

Pippin did a double take, staring at me like he just didn't believe I was inside the costume.

'That is uncanny,' he murmured.

Barbie agreed. 'I know, right? It's amazing.'

Pippin fitted the earpiece, tucking the wire behind my ear and down the back of my dress.

'Are you all right in there, Mrs Fisher?' he asked. 'You seem a little ... damp.'

'It's hot as hell inside this thing,' I moaned. 'Are we done? I need to get this over with before I pass out.'

'Sure, you're all set to go.' Pippin backed away, returning to his post after giving me a rough lie of the land.

Barbie led the way into the Tiki Bar, taking eyes off me because, well, everyone looks at Barbie. Young or old, man or woman, though to be fair mostly the women are looking to try to figure out what their husbands were gawping at.

I spotted Schneider first, easy because he was standing up and that made him the tallest person in the bar. He was chatting with two women roughly his own age while surreptitiously keeping an eye on our mark. I spotted Ricardo next, but then I already knew he was sitting at the bar. Deepa was next to him, filling the space so that I could arrive and find an available chair as she vacated it.

'I'm heading for the bar now, Deepa,' I spoke naturally, hoping it would pick up my voice even with the noise of conversation around me.

Her voice arrived in my right ear a half second later.

'Roger. I'm ready to move.'

I came in from behind her, counting down as I approached so she could time her dismount and leave the barstool free for me. Smooth, that's how we were going to do this.

'Three. Two. One.'

Deepa picked up her drink, sticking her clutch bag under one arm and the straw in her mouth as she rotated clockwise to plant her feet on the deck. I was a yard away and about to ask if the barstool was free when Deepa raised a hand to block my path.

'Sorry, I'm saving this for someone,' she said, looking over my shoulders and around. 'She'll be here any second.' she didn't recognise me either – the disguise was just too good.

'It's me,' I hissed at her, my voice coming through her radio as well as the fact that I was standing almost toe to toe with her.

She looked at me, her head tilting to one side.

'I'm a lonely old widow, bored with sitting in my cabin all alone and hoped I might find some company in one of this ship's fine bars,' I gabbled my lines, hoping Deepa would come to her senses and let me sit down.

Ricardo swivelled in his chair, looking around to see what was happening.

Looking directly at Deepa, I hissed insistently, 'It's Patricia.' Except, of course, I didn't. Trying hard to not blow our cover by making a big scene right next to the target, I forgot about the teeth and spat them out on the P of my name just as I had every time so far.

They flew through the air, and I lunged to catch them. This time though, Deepa was too close, and my hand hit her first. The teeth were heading for her cleavage, the plunge of her cocktail dress providing the perfect spot for them to vanish. My hand performed an uppercut on her left breast, popping it up and then out of her dress as my teeth splatted against her skin, leaving a blob of saliva as they bounced off and onto the floor.

A man sitting a yard away burst out laughing, nudging the man sitting next to him and nodded at Deepa's exposed embarrassment. He shut up a second later when his wife scowled at him.

Ricardo was eyeing me with deep mistrust as Deepa yanked her dress back into place and moved out of the way. She was heading out of the bar – unhappy to stay now she had been unexpectedly showing off her goods.

'Hello,' I shot the Italian a smile. 'Do you mind if I sit here? I'm awfully lonely and you have a kind face.'

He wasn't buying a word of it.

'What happened to your teeth?' he asked, his expression a mask of concern. He was looking at my neck and I realised that though Sixpence and Madrigal had covered me as best they could, my neck was one bit of me where the skin still showed through, and he could see that the parts of me were not adding up.

'What is this?' he asked. 'What's going on?' He was looking around, worry filling his face.

I was losing him. Giving it all I had, I pulled a wad of money from my purse. It was tantamount to entrapment, but I was losing him if I didn't.

'I am happy to pay for you to keep me company,' I told him. Then when he looked at my face, I gave him a saucy wink that was supposed to infer all manner of suggestions.

Quick as a flash, he turned to the barman, snatched his wallet from an inside back pocket and thrust a one hundred dollar bill at him.

'Keep the change,' he instructed, making the barman's day as Ricardo turned away from me and started toward the door.

I swore under my breath, though it was loud enough for my team to hear.

'What's happening?' asked Sam, failing to keep up with events. I hadn't been able to spot him until now, but he was on his feet, watching our target escape. Wearing white shorts and a Hawaiian shirt in blue and yellow he was starting to follow. So too were Schneider and Baker.

'Give me a minute, guys,' I begged them. 'This is a total bust, but maybe I can salvage it. Just hang back and be ready if I call for you, okay?'

I got a chorus of reluctant agreement as the guys moved slowly toward the bar entrance where they would wait.

Ricardo was already going out of it, and I was hot on his heels.

'I know you killed Evelyn,' I called after him, expecting my bold statement to stop him dead in his tracks. He just kept going though, forcing me to power on despite the stabbing pain in my feet. The tights had shifted too, riding up rather than falling down so it now felt like my crotch was spring loaded. On top of that, I was sweating so profusely I could feel it gathering in the small of my back and my cleavage where the bandages stopped it from escaping. They were getting ever tighter, and I was gasping my breaths now as I hurried after the Italian gigolo.

'It wasn't your fault, was it?' I shouted as best I could, sounding breathless.

He ignored me, walking at a pace, but making no attempt to run.

'Mrs Fisher, where are you?' Baker asked.

I ignored him, desperate to get one case in the bag since a solution to the Oswalds' investigation continued to elude me.

'Mr Rossini, I am the ship's detective,' I wheezed. 'It is better for you to come clean and tell me what happened to Evelyn Goodwin.' We were right by the indoor pool set at the bottom of the opening in the middle of the ship. Light and air spilled into the ship, plunging down several decks to fill them with sunshine in the daytime.

I worried he might run, my recent poolside chases having all ended badly for me, but he stopped abruptly, spinning around to glare at me.

'Who is this Evelyn woman you speak of? I don't know anyone called Evelyn. You are some kind of prankster, yes? Dressing up to play tricks on an innocent man having a drink. Who are you really?'

Sparkly lights were beginning to dance in front of my eyes as heat and lack of oxygen clawed at my consciousness.

'I'm,' I started to tell him my name, but stopped because saying 'Patricia' would eject my silly fake teeth. Then I remembered they were already gone, and I could speak normally. I tried again, 'I'm ...' What did I need to say next?

My legs didn't feel like they were attached to my body, and I got a strange sensation of movement as I staggered to one side. Something rubbed against my right shin. My eyesight was fading, a clanging sound filling my ears as rushing blood robbed another of my senses.

I needed to sit down, that's all. Get my head between my knees, find a way to get the bandages around my chest to loosen, and I would be fine. I just needed a minute. There were sunbeds here, lots of them. I would just park myself on one of those.

I heard Ricardo say something, but the sound was all fuzzy and messed up, like he was speaking from a long way off or from inside a cardboard box.

It sounded like, 'Hey, watch out for the pool,' but whatever it was that he did say made no difference because I was suddenly falling.

When I came to, however many minutes later it was, I wasn't in the pool, I was on a sunbed. My clothing was loose, and I could breathe. My wig was gone, so too my shoes, but I remembered hitting the water and I was very clearly soaking wet now.

What happened after I fell into the pool though?

The sound of running feet drew my eyes around to the right. Barbie was in the lead, obviously. Still wearing Lycra and running shoes, she was twice as fast as anyone else, but Deepa was only just a short way behind, one arm across her chest to pin her boobs down as she ran to get to me. The others were on her tail, Sam bringing up the rear, but looking every bit as concerned as everyone else.

'Mrs Fisher, what happened?' gasped Lieutenant Commander Baker.

I lifted my head and looked around at the pool tile.

'I would guess I fell in, and Ricardo jumped in to save me.' I could come up with no other explanation. He had been the only one around. He fished me out, loosened the bindings around my chest, and ran off before anyone could discover him.

'You were mumbling into the radio,' Baker told me. 'Not making any sense. Then the transmission went dead.'

'That must have been when you fell in the pool, Mrs Fisher,' said Sam, proud that he had worked it out.

'It must have been,' I agreed. This was a fine pickle. I was trying to lure the man into admitting his crimes and instead he saved my life. I owed him one, for sure, but I couldn't let him off the hook, it wasn't my decision to make.

'It didn't sound like you got anything out of him,' Deepa observed.

I shook my head. 'No, he wasn't giving anything away. He's bright enough to know that we don't know anything.'

I lifted one sodden arm, watching water run off it before I let it fall back to my lap with a splat noise.

'I need to get cleaned up again,' I moaned at myself. How many times had I changed my clothes today? 'Let's regroup in a little while, shall we? I'm sure everyone needs some dinner.'

Most of them had eaten a late lunch just like me so were not hungry, but there wasn't anything I could think of to do about any of our cases, so the team was going to relax for a while, and I was going to slog back to my suite to get dressed.

'I'll go with you,' Barbie volunteered. 'You look like a homeless person right now and I don't want concerned passengers trying to save you.'

She gave me a hand up, but it was much easier walking now that I didn't have the granny shoes on. Remembering my pool session prior to this one, I told Barbie about borrowing her boots and what had happened to them.

She was quite generous about it, possibly because we had just patched things up after the incident with the email. She hadn't worn them in a long time, she claimed. I hoped she was telling the truth and not secretly sore that I had ruined them.

As it so often does, my brain was still trying to figure things out, and the randomly colliding electrons in my head supplied a ridiculous idea.

'Plan B,' I murmured to myself.

Barbie twitched her head around. 'Hmm? Did you say something?'

'Oh, just thinking aloud,' I replied.

‘Then why are you rubbing your hands together like the Grinch about to steal Christmas?’

I glanced down to find I was doing precisely that. Dropping my hands back to my sides, I said, ‘I just had a thought about something that might help to catch Ricardo. I don’t think I can have another go at it.’ I needed to make a call.

Call From Sam

The dogs ran over to see me the moment I came through the door, took one look at the water still dripping off my clothes and ran back to the couch again.

Jermaine handed me a towel and held two more ready if I needed them. I'd gotten a lot of funny looks trudging back through the ship to my suite, but thankfully, my disguise meant they wouldn't recognise me the next time I walked by.

I patted myself dry, then jogged briskly to my bedroom where, in the bathroom, I stripped and threw the wet items into the bath. I didn't need to get clean, but I took a shower anyway, washing off the chlorine and sweat so I would feel more human when I went out to face the world again.

Leaving the bathroom and shutting the door to trap the steam inside, I found a balloon glass of gin and tonic waiting for me on my dressing table. It was right in front of my stool and worked wonders to change my mood.

I shouted loud enough to be heard in the main part of the suite.

'Jermaine, I love you!' I took another gulp and questioned what there was that I could do today that I had not already done. I was feeling fatigued, and no wonder – the day had been a full-on adventure from start to finish.

The Oswalds' jewellery theft case appeared to be back at the start. Betty Ross couldn't have done it because she had a perfect and irrefutable alibi ... the back of my skull itched. She did have a perfect alibi. She had an answer to every question. Her jacket, the one that was seen on the camera in Arthur English's jewellery store could be bought on board which meant almost everyone – every woman of a certain age at least –

could buy one and pose as her. The halter neck top was a fairly generic one and the jacket hid most of it.

Earlier, down in the brig when she was being released, all my thoughts had been about figuring out who her accomplice was. She had been careful to have an airtight alibi, and I assumed she knew we would find evidence pointing toward her at some point.

So what was I saying?

My phone rang, Sam's name showing on the screen when I looked. I parked my train of thought, promising I would come back and pick it up again in a minute.

'Hey, Sam, what's up?' I asked, putting the phone on speaker as I opened my underwear drawer to select a pair of knickers.

'Hi, Mrs Fisher,' he gushed in his usual exuberant manner. 'There's an Italian man here.'

He was still trying to crack the case, bless him, not fully grasping the subtle part where we needed to find the right Italian man, not just any man from Italy. I was about to tell him to come to my cabin to play with the dogs, when he said something else.

'He's on his way to a cabin with granny. He gave me fifty bucks to stay in the bar,' he sounded thrilled at the prospect, but my heart thumped in my chest and my skull started to itch like mad. 'Do you want a drink?' he asked. It explained why he was calling – he had money and was by himself in a bar, not a great combination.

'Sam,' I licked my lips, an unconscious action as I prayed I was about to catch a break. 'Sam, did you happen to hear the man's name.'

'Yes,' Sam chortled. 'His name is Claude.'

I punched the air and tried to put my knickers on so fast they tangled in my toes, and I fell over. Jermaine must have heard the thump, because he was knocking on my door two seconds later.

'Madam, is everything all right?'

Now on my back, I kicked my legs into the air and wriggled my bottom. Bouncing back onto my feet, I now had one item of clothing on.

'Yes! Everything is fine. We have to go out. Right now!' I yelled, fumbling for my bra. 'Sam, what bar are you in?'

'The Tiki Bar. It's fun in here. They have an inflatable palm tree!'

'Yes, they do,' I acknowledged. 'Do you know where your granny went? Which direction and how long ago did they leave?' I shimmied my backside, probably looking like someone dancing when utterly drunk. But no one could see me and now I had jeans on.

While Sam relayed the next pieces of information and I sent him to carefully tail where his granny had gone, I stuffed my feet into a pair of running shoes and snagged a t-shirt from my closet. I was almost there.

My hair was a mess, but by the time Barbie ran into my room to check what was happening, I had a ballcap holding my damp blonde locks in place. Makeup be damned, I was going as I was, wrinkles and all.

'Should I call Deepa and the others?' Barbie asked as I grabbed her shoulders, shoved her toward the door, and pushed her out ahead of me.

'No time!' I barked.

My dachshunds, Anna and Georgie, spun on the spot, excited because the humans were excited and bouncing from paw to paw in their haste to get out of the door.

I wasn't going to take them, but at the last moment figured they might make for a good cover – I was just a person out walking my dogs.

At the door, Jermaine was shucking his butler's set of tails.

'You're coming too?' Barbie asked, grabbing the door handle as I clipped the dogs to their leads.

Jermaine checked his reflection in the mirror as he ripped off his bow tie. Without the jacket and tie, he just looked like a man in a shirt and trousers. A tall, muscular, Jamaican man in a shirt and trousers, but far less noticeable than he had been a moment ago.

To answer Barbie, he said, 'Mrs Fisher can, at times, find her way into situations that can be … threatening.'

'You mean downright dangerous,' I corrected him, swinging out of the door and starting to run.

Sam was still on the end of the phone, though I had expressly instructed him to not put it on speaker.

'Sam, where are you now? Can you see your Gran?'

He took a moment to respond and in my head, I could picture him playing secret agents; hiding from sight and peering around a corner as he tailed Gloria and the Italian man.

'Gran is just ahead, Mrs Fisher,' he replied in his usual jovial manner. 'Oh, hold on. They just stopped. It looks like gran is getting some money from the ATM.'

Exactly as I expected and the itching sensation inside my skull subsided because I had just figured it out.

'Who are we after?' asked Barbie. 'Is it Ricardo again?'

We were running, though it was more of a jog, but fast enough that I was having to choose between breathing and talking. Barbie and Jermaine had no such conflict of interests - they could both speak quite easily despite the exertion.

I shook my head and managed to blurt, 'His brother.'

'Brother?' Barbie questioned. 'I thought Pippin said he was travelling with his husband.'

I nodded and stopped running. We were a minute or more from where we needed to be, but as long as I got to Gloria before she and Claude got down to um ... business – I figured I had enough time to slow down to a walking pace and I needed to if I was going to talk.

The dachshunds tried to carry on running – they thought this was a great game. Jermaine reached out a hand to take the leads from me and I passed them over.

Grabbing a lungful of air, I said, 'That's where I went wrong right at the start. Pippin spotted Ricardo with Evelyn and Priscilla; I could have wrapped the whole thing up yesterday, but I figured two men travelling together with the same name must be a gay couple.'

Barbie saw it instantly. 'But they are brothers. That's why their name is the same and they are here to earn money by offering their unique service to the ladies onboard.'

'They are not the first to think of it. If they were, we wouldn't all know the word gigolo.'

Jermaine commented, 'It comes from the French word gigolette which means a woman of the streets, which in turn is probably a derivative of the word giguer which means to frolic. Gigolo is simply the masculine version of the same term.'

Barbie and I stopped talking and stared at him.

'What?' he asked, frowning. 'I can know things.'

We were still walking at a pace, getting closer to where I believed we would find Sam when I heard him gasp. It was a sudden intake of breath, the kind one makes when sucker punched in the gut. It was followed by the sound of him retching and coughing, the noises of distress enough to get all three of us running without any need for words.

'Sam!' I yelled into my phone.

What I got in response was what sounded like expletives uttered in Italian and the line went dead.

Sam was in trouble! Sam was in trouble, and I didn't know where he was. Had he stayed in the same place? Who was it that we just heard? Was it Ricardo? Had he figured out we were onto his sex ring and come to warn his brother? Why wouldn't he just phone it in?

The answer swam into my brain - because he went in the pool to rescue you and probably killed his phone in the process.

Haring around a corner, terrified for what I might find, we found Sam on the ground being tended to by a dozen concerned passengers and two members of crew.

We had to fight our way through, discovering that Sam was trying desperately to get up only to be pinned in place by someone who believed he needed to stay down until medical help arrived.

'Get Sam!' I yelled to Jermaine, taking the dog leads from him. There was no time for explanations, but I slapped a crewmember, a woman in her thirties in steward's livery, on the shoulder, shouting, 'Call security! Send them after us!'

There was no time for anything else. The Rossinis had a hostage, if that was their plan for Gloria, and could be heading anywhere. The ship is a big place if people want to hide. We would dock in Lanzarote during the night meaning they only had to hide out for a few hours and maybe they could then find a way to escape. I couldn't guess what was in their minds, but a dozen terrible scenarios played out, each one holding more potential horror than the one before.

Ahead of me, Barbie came across a couple on their way to dinner. She screeched to a stop, blocking their path, and startling them.

'An old lady and two well-dressed men in their fifties – did you see them in the last minute? Did they come by you?' Her words came with enough urgency to prompt an immediate response.

'Yes,' blurted the woman, swinging around to look back the way she had come. 'They were in an awful hurry.'

'They were heading outside, I think,' added the man.

Barbie shot around them, shouting her thanks over her shoulder as she sprinted down the passageway.

The short delay had given Jermaine enough time to catch up, charging up behind me with Sam in tow. My assistant had a hand to his gut, confirming one of the brothers had hit him.

Five seconds later, I got there too, leaving the ship's structure to find myself on the deck. The warm air off the African coast blew at my hair, loose strands tickling my face where they had escaped the ball cap.

I didn't need to look for Barbie, she was five yards away and standing still. She couldn't move because ahead of her, the Rossini brothers were holding knives.

Hostage Negotiation

Barbie's hands were splayed wide apart to show she had nothing in them, but the threat wasn't really aimed at her. Between the Rossini brothers, Gloria hung limply. Ricardo and Claude had a hand each gripping her biceps to hold her in place, and they were brandishing blades – wicked looking fold-out butterfly knives that they should not have been able to smuggle on board.

'Let's not do anything silly,' Barbie implored.

Ricardo flicked his eyes to me as I came onto the deck behind her, performing a shocked double take when he realised who I was.

'That was quite the costume earlier, lady. You had me fooled,' he admitted. 'I didn't know until I saw your neck, and even then, it wasn't until your wig fell off that I realised what was going on.' Talking to his brother in quick-fire Italian, not that he took his eyes off me, he said something I didn't understand.

Both men had panic in their eyes, the look of criminals who know they have been cornered and are looking for any way out. Any way at all.

Jermaine and Sam spread out to my left and right, four of us now focused on the Rossini brothers. Anna and Georgie, my miniature dachshunds who weigh about ten pounds each, stretched to the end of their leads and growled menacingly.

Sam asked, 'Are you okay, Gran?'

Claude jerked Gloria's arm, preventing her from replying so that he could make his demands.

'There's a helicopter onboard. We want a pilot in ten minutes. We are flying out of here and we are taking the old lady for insurance.'

'That's not going to happen,' I assured him, trying to make myself sound like a hostage negotiator even though I was about ready to wet my knickers. 'The charges against you are minimal. If you surrender now, there might not even be any jail time.'

Ricardo spat on the deck, his face a mask of rage.

'You're going to pin that woman's death on me! That's what this is about! Well, I didn't kill her. I couldn't have known she had a weak heart.'

'I know,' I agreed, offering him a sympathetic face. 'I believe you. You were horrified, weren't you?' I was trying to recall a film I'd seen where the negotiator was trying to win the trust of the maniac holding the bomb and threatening to kill a bus load of tourists. I needed to calm him down, that was the first thing.

'She's stalling!' snarled Claude. 'There will be snipers on the bridge if we don't hurry up. She doesn't believe what she is saying. She's just lining us up to be shot.'

'No, I'm not!' I protested. Ignoring Claude to focus on Ricardo, I said, 'You positioned Evelyn, didn't you? It was tender and loving because you are right; you couldn't know she had a weak heart. You must have helped so many ladies during your time onboard, giving them something they thought they would never have again.'

Okay, so now I didn't believe what I was saying, but I was playing the role of hostage negotiator and doing my best to defuse the situation.

'Helicopter! Now!' bellowed Claude.

I kept my eyes on Ricardo. 'If you leave here with a hostage, you will be on the run for the rest of your lives. If you surrender, you will be arrested, but what crime have you actually committed?'

From the corner of her mouth, Barbie hissed, 'They're holding a woman at knifepoint, Patty.'

I hissed back, 'Shhhh!' and continued to talk Ricardo off the proverbial ledge. 'How many women have you 'helped' since you came onboard, Ricardo?' I asked.

He sagged just a little, his grip around Gloria's arm loosening a fraction as doubt seeped into his mind.

'Lots,' he admitted. 'Too many to count. Lonely older women are everywhere, and they are happy to pay me for my company.'

'Mine too,' pointed out his brother, feeling left out.

'Is that enough?' asked Gloria, speaking for the first time and startling the brothers with how calm she sounded.

I nodded my head, satisfied that I had all I needed.

'Yes, I should think so.'

With no warning whatsoever, Gloria whipped her right arm upward. She caught Ricardo off guard, her arm getting up past her waist before he even sensed her moving. He tightened his grip, but by then it was too late. The handbag, at the end of Gloria's arm and gathering speed as it whipped through a wide arc, smacked Claude in the face like a wrecking ball.

The blow contained enough power that his grip faltered, and his arm fell away. Now free on one side, while Claude tottered and had a good think about falling over, Gloria switched her bag into her free hand and reversed her swing.

Jermaine had exploded into action the second he saw what was happening. He was too far away to stop the first blow from landing but could have stopped the second. Which means he made a conscious decision not to. It made me love him just a little bit more.

Gloria went for the low blow, her handbag, complete with house brick, struck Ricardo between his legs with such force that it almost lifted him from the deck.

Sam screwed up his face and made a wincing sound even as he raced to give Jermaine a hand to rescue his granny.

Not that Gloria needed rescuing. She had been my plan B all along. With a slightly nuts octogenarian at my disposal, why wouldn't I employ her when she happily volunteered? Of course, she wasn't supposed to get snatched and menaced with a knife. In fact, she wasn't really supposed to do anything. I called her earlier to find out what she had planned for her evening and asked her to be on the lookout for any handsome Italian men in their fifties. She went to a bar most nights and she fit the demographic – I was kind of surprised she hadn't run into them already.

I then had to explain why I was making my request and send her photographs of the Rossinis, but she was supposed to do exactly as I had planned – draw them into revealing what they were doing on the Aurelia and hopefully take cash from her. My instructions were to message me the moment she met them so I could arrange for someone to be there to watch her and keep her safe.

It worked a little too well, albeit she found Ricardo's brother instead. She'd placed herself in harm's way, but with Barbie and Sam following hard on Jermaine's heels, any danger to Gloria was thankfully removed.

Claude stopped tottering when he lost his battle for consciousness. His nose was spread across his face, blood running from it to stain the white of his shirt. Ricardo was in a foetal position on the deck, his hands cupping his wotsits while he moaned and groaned.

Thundering feet from the passageway behind me turning into half a dozen members of the ship's security team a moment later when they burst through the door and onto the deck. The dachshunds spun around to face the latest threat, barking and snapping at the ship's security with the same gusto they had aimed at the Rossinis.

'Hello, chaps,' I gave them a pinky wave. 'Two for the brig, I believe. Or maybe sick bay. There're some wounds to tend.'

With the security team there to take over, I grabbed Sam by his arm, pulling him to one side.

'How are you feeling, Sam?' I wanted to know. He was being looked after by his granny. Gloria is lovely and dotes on Sam, but she could also be relied upon to be tipsy on gin half the time. I was compensating for the absence of his mother whether I needed to or not and I knew he had been hurt by Ricardo.

'I'm all right, Mrs Fisher,' he grinned and gave me thumbs up. 'It takes more than a punch to the gut to ruin my Dunkirk spirit.'

Well, I rather liked that. His attitude was can-do, and I knew he'd picked it up from Jermaine.

'Is it dinnertime?' he asked, rubbing his stomach though I couldn't be sure if that was to signify it was empty or because it hurt still.

'Coo, yes,' agreed Gloria, 'some dinner sounds wonderful. What are we having?'

'You know,' I put my arm around his shoulders to steer him back toward the ship's structure and then my cabin. 'I think we should have whatever Sam and Gloria want. They saved the day, after all.'

Gloria remarked, 'Good thing too. That pair have been costing me a fortune since they came on board.'

Before we could get back inside fresh footsteps hurrying our way heralded the arrival of Lieutenant Commander Baker and his team, all four of them arriving at a pace. Baker thanked a colleague, one of the other security guards who had arrived first on the scene a few minutes ago, then headed straight for me.

'We heard you got into a little bother,' he remarked, explaining their presence – someone radioed my team.

'No bother,' I replied. 'My apologies for not calling you, there just didn't seem to be time.'

The team was looking about, Schneider and Pippin checking with the chaps who arrived first, but there was nothing for them to do. Evidence would be gathered to tie up the case with a neat bow, but it was snatching Gloria at knifepoint that would put the gigolos behind bars.

'Well,' chuckled Deepa, 'at least you didn't have to put on a disguise this time.'

I laughed too. But only for a second. My face froze as my skull started itching again.

'The whole thing was a disguise,' I murmured, talking to myself. My hands moved fast, yanking my phone from a back pocket.

'What was a disguise? asked Deepa as I passed her.

From behind me Barbie's voice rang out, 'Patty? Patty where are you going?'

My feet were operating of their own accord – they knew where they needed to go and could get me there without the need of my brain. My brain was doing other things and my eyes were scrutinising the picture of

Betty Ross in the jewellery store. My Grinch leer was back, curling the corners of my mouth as a deep sense of satisfaction settled over me.

In my wake, and just about making it into my consciousness so I knew they were there, I could hear everyone else following gamely and discussing me.

Sam and Gloria, Barbie and Jermaine, and all four of my security team - they were willing to let me get on with it or were just used to my oddness. Whichever it was, I was the topic of discussion. Or rather, my need to be cryptic was.

I didn't need to be cryptic. I didn't even intend to be. Well, all right, sometimes I did, but this wasn't one of them.

I'd just figured out the gold digger case.

Maybe.

The picture was inconclusive – it would never hold up in court, so I needed a confession. Fortunately, I knew just how I was going to test my theory before I went full-throttle and started accusing people.

'Should we ask her where we are going?' Gloria asked, her voice penetrating my brain but not enough that I really heard her. I was trying to sift through the fog of clues in my head, and there weren't any, not really. Somehow though, I knew I was right.

'Are we going to her suite?' asked Pippin, guessing right as we came into the passageway that led to my accommodation.

Taking a break from my internal plotting, I took out my keycard and swiped at the panel to open the door.

'You guys can wait here,' I told them. 'I won't be a second.' When I emerged again roughly a minute later, the dachshunds were settled on the couch once more and I had collected the thing I needed.

Barbie observed, 'That was quick.' Like everyone else now looking my way, she wanted to know what I had gone into the suite for. I wasn't telling though. Not yet.

We set off again, heading for the Platinum Suite. Coming toward my destination, I reached for my handbag – I wanted my universal key because I wasn't going to ask if I could enter first. I hadn't taken my handbag with me though, a small fact that slipped my mind until I tried to open it.

'Anyone got a key?' I twisted around to direct the question at the four security officers.

'Ah, yes, Mrs Fisher,' replied Baker, 'we all have. Do we have just cause to enter? Can we knock instead?' Bursting into passenger cabins required paperwork to be filed and eyebrows would be raised at Purple Star HQ if we couldn't justify our actions. Baker was doing his job and trying to make sure I did mine.

I smiled, playing nicely. In my head I was Bruce Willis with boobs and this situation required an explosion or something.

Instead, I reached out with one hand and rapped my knuckles politely on the door of the Platinum Suite. We had to wait almost a minute – butlers will not be hurried – but Bartholomew opened the door and filled the frame with his body.

The scent of gin was on the air, my nose picking it out from the other background smells. It made me want one, but there would be time for that soon enough.

‘Good evening, Mrs Fisher. I’m afraid Mr Oswald is not at home.’

‘That’s okay,’ I cut him off and squeezed through the gap left between his body and the doorframe – a butler would never put an arm out to stop a person unless they truly, truly needed to. ‘I’m not here to see him.’

‘I beg your pardon, Mrs Fisher!’ Bartholomew expressed his indignant rage as only a butler could. Of course, in turning around to track where I was going, he made an even bigger gap for everyone else to follow me into the suite. ‘This is outrageous!’ he complained.

Jermaine flapped a dismissive arm at the man, ‘Oh, put a sock in it, Bartie. Let Mrs Fisher do her job and she’ll be out of your hair soon enough. Or are you involved in the thefts?’ he asked, shocking the staid Englishman.

The last I saw, as I glanced back across the room, was Bartholomew’s shocked mouth hanging slackly open.

The words, ‘How dare you?’ filled the room, but I was already pushing Tulisa’s door open.

‘What the heck?’ she was on her bed, but bouncing off it to repel whoever was coming in by the time I got the door open far enough to see her. ‘Get out!’ she shrieked. ‘This is my room!’

I moved my right hand up to scratch an imaginary itch on my neck and watched her eyes as they twitched down to see what I was doing. This was where I got my answer. I was right or I was wrong.

Tulisa saw the five-carat sapphire necklace hanging around my neck and her eyes gave the game away.

‘You didn’t expect to see this again, did you?’ I asked.

'Get out!' she screamed in my face, and when I didn't move, she snatched up her phone from the bed. 'I'm calling my father!'

'Good,' I nodded. 'He ought to hear this,' I agreed.

Her fingers paused just above the screen, trembling in mid-air as she tried to decide what to do.

A fresh kerfuffle from outside told me John Oswald was back and it didn't surprise me to hear Betty's voice too. They had arrived back at their suite to find it filled with people like an impromptu party had been arranged without anyone telling them.

'What's going on?' John demanded to know. 'Someone had better start talking,' he insisted in a voice that was used to getting what it wanted.

I stepped back into the main living space of the suite.

'Hello again, Mr Oswald. Sorry to interrupt, it really couldn't wait, I'm afraid. I'm just clearing up the matter of the thefts.'

His forehead creased into a frown, his eyes flicking from my face to his granddaughter's room where she still hid inside.

He asked, 'What are you doing in Tulisa's room?' As a question it was as obvious as it was dumb.

Tulisa shouted a response, 'Invading my privacy! I could have been getting changed and she burst in with her goons. She didn't even knock!'

I let a smile play across my face as I turned around to face her again.

'You saw Betty's jacket and bought one just like it, didn't you?' Not waiting for an answer, for my question was rhetorical, I fiddled with my phone until the picture Arthur English emailed me popped up. I twisted it to show her and watched her pupils dilate.

'You didn't know there was a camera, did you?' Another rhetorical question.

Tulisa regained her composure faster than I expected. 'What is this?' she demanded. 'That's not me. It doesn't look anything like me.'

John had let go of Betty's hand to bustle his way across the room.

'What is all this, Mrs Fisher? What is going on?'

I turned the screen so he could see it, and we all had to wait while he fiddled in his pockets to find his reading glasses.

'Throw them out, Granddad,' Tulisa demanded. 'They've no right to be in here accusing me of anything.'

'That looks like you, Betty,' exclaimed John, peering over the top of his glasses at his girlfriend. Betty had followed him across the room and was looking at the screen too.

'Yes, it does, doesn't it?' I agreed. 'It was the single piece of evidence on which I chose to arrest her earlier today. It looks exactly like her, which begs me to question why you didn't say that when I showed it to you, Tulisa?'

Tulisa's next words caught in her throat.

'You didn't try to tell me it was Miss Ross because you already know the woman in the photograph is you.'

'This is utter nonsense,' Tulisa laughed a fake laugh. 'Anyone can see that isn't me. I don't dress like that ...'

'Clothes are easily changed,' I argued. 'You will have discarded the pink jacket, of course, probably before you got back on the ship, but what is the likelihood that I will find a receipt logged against your credit card at the boutique that sells it?'

She didn't know the answer to that one and was looking distinctly less certain now.

'Look at her boobs,' Tulisa sneered, cupping her own breasts to show how meagre they were by comparison. 'These aren't inflatable, you know.' She made the comment as if she were cracking a joke at my expense.

I simply shook my head in a sad way. 'That's the easiest part of the disguise to fake, Tulisa.'

'That's not my hair,' she tried.

I countered it easily. 'A wig. Also discarded, but my team will find hair from it on your clothing or on the carpet or bed. Or maybe in your bag, but they will find it.' I refused to blink or look away, pinning her in place with my eyes. 'None of that really matters though, because I have all I need in the photograph.'

I turned through ninety degrees to face John again. Using forefinger and thumb, I zoomed into the picture, bringing the right eyebrow into focus. The image was a little grainy, but clear enough for me to see the hole where a piercing would normally be. I then shifted the picture to show the one in her lip. It was in the exact same place as the piercing Tulisa now wore and right next to a birthmark. It might not get a conviction in court, but I doubted I would need that.

'Scar tissue is one thing that is hard to fake,' I remarked, my tone almost apologetic.

Tulisa had no comeback. There was no argument she could pose that would get her off now. So she didn't even try, opting instead to go on the offensive.

'Yeah, well, it's not stealing, is it!' she shouted. 'It's my money, they are my jewels. I am due to inherit all of it! Dad only gives me ten thousand dollars a week pocket money. How am I supposed to live on that?'

'Oh, Tulisa,' gasped John, looking at his granddaughter as if he hardly recognised her.

So far as the case was concerned, we were done and could close the file. Tulisa was right that there was no crime. Neither John nor Tim were going to press criminal charges. This was a family matter, and they could sort it out for themselves.

Reluctantly, I lifted both hands to my neck, removing the sapphire necklace.

'How did it come to be in your possession?' John Oswald wanted to know.

'My boyfriend bought it for me,' I replied as I placed it in his palm. 'It is a family heirloom and I think it should stay with the family.' Locking eyes with the patriarch, I added, 'I think you might want to keep it out of her grasp for a few years though.'

Tulisa was going to protest until she saw the thunder in her grandfather's face. She withered, skulking off to sit on her bed where she put headphones on and did a rather good job of pretending the rest of us were not there.

To Betty, I said, 'I hope you can understand why I thought it was you earlier.'

'There are no hard feelings,' she replied, generously letting me off the hook. 'I'm just glad it is all sorted out so that Tim can make peace with his father. We need him to be best man.'

'You're getting married,' I blurted, my cheeks colouring when I realised how I had said it. 'I'm sorry. I didn't mean for it to come out like that.'

John Oswald laughed. 'That's all right, Mrs Fisher. It's a little sudden, I know. I guess I don't think I have a lot of time to wait around and figure things out. At my age you tend to go with your gut. I do, at least.'

'Congratulations,' I offered them a smile that contained genuine warmth. Love sure is an odd thing. 'If you need a high-end wedding planner ...' It was a throwaway comment but one which the couple latched onto.

'You know someone?' Betty asked. 'We want to get married on the ship.'

Now on the spot, I questioned what Felicity Phillips might say when I called her later. It was the kind of lavish, expensive, over the top affair she catered for, but how full would her diary be? I was going to have to find out if the expectant faces looking at me now were anything to go by.

I couldn't stop the voices shouting inside my head. Betty Ross, by her own mother's admission, was a light-fingered individual who used her looks to gain advantage. Was she running a scam now? I had to search my feelings and gave myself a second to form an opinion. The truth was that I thought she was genuine. I couldn't tell John, it just wouldn't be fair, but I would be watching.

A few minutes later, and promising I would call the wedding planner as soon as business hours open in England, I left the suite with my entourage in tow.

It was time for a gin.

I asked everyone to come to my suite for there was something to discuss. I would get that out of the way first, because once that was done, I had a plan for my evening. All in all, the day had turned out better than expected. Two of the three cases were wrapped up and I had never expected to get very far with the stowaway case anyway.

Murder

On the other side of the Atlantic, in a Rio de Janeiro backstreet, Xavier Silvestre wiped the blood from his knife and put it away, catching a glimpse of his reflection in a puddle when he moved. Even he couldn't recognise who it was under the makeup.

Silvestre enjoyed disguises. He liked how they allowed him to be someone different and how he could change his appearance completely with a few simple prosthetics.

Today, his left hand was an articulated claw – an old thing he picked up on the internet many years ago. With a wig, some makeup, and the simple addition of tatty clothing, he stopped being a multi-millionaire treasure hunter and transformed into a doddery homeless man with a missing left hand.

People wouldn't remember him, but should the police ever try to find Antonio Bardem's killer and found anyone who remembered seeing anything, it would be the old, homeless man they sought.

Killing the greedy museum assistant had been easy; the fool never saw it coming. Once Silvestre dangled a wad of cash under the man's nose, Bardem told him everything he knew and even escorted him to where the man who brought in the cross was staying.

Bardem had never met Silvestre before, so had no idea he wasn't seeing the real man. All he saw was the money, which Silvestre took back after he plunged a knife into Bardem's neck. Then he emptied the research assistant's pockets, making it look like a robbery/homicide.

It wasn't his first murder, not by a long way and it was necessary – no one could know what had been found. He would go to the museum next once Carlos Ramirez had told him where he found the cross.

An hour later, Xavier Silvestre walked out of the hotel with all the information Carlos had known now safely tucked away where no one else could ever discover it. He wore another disguise, this time an overweight man in his forties with a pot belly hanging over his belt, a balding head, and a fat cigar poking from his mouth – it was the small things that made his disguises so complete. Again, there was little chance they would remember him, and if they did, they would be looking for a man who didn't exist.

By the time they found Ramirez's body, Silvestre would be on his private plane over the Atlantic or safely in another country.

'The Aurelia,' Carlos had croaked, unable to believe how his life had changed. An hour ago, he believed he was on the cusp of making a pot of money. Now he was trying to stay alive.

The fat man with the stinking cigar wouldn't kill him if he thought there was more to learn – Carlos was quite literally betting his life on that principle. He explained that he met an albino through a friend of a friend – mostly true – and that the scruffy Irishman had an uncut diamond in his possession that was the size of a man's thumb.

Sweating inside the fat suit he wore, Silvestre listened to Ramirez. He could tell the man was lying about some of what he was revealing, but he also believed much of it was true.

Murphy, an Irishman if Ramirez could be believed, had stumbled upon the gems when he was looking for fossils. It was a crazy story he might have refused to believe if Ramirez hadn't attempted to keep hold of it even while being tortured.

Carlos lied about where it took place, claiming to have been in Morocco at the time. He was nowhere near Morocco when they met. He wasn't even on that continent, but Carlos believed he could survive this encounter. If he escaped with the truth intact, he now knew for certain that the albino had found something very valuable. Why else would the fat man be going to such extremes to learn about him.

Carlos almost killed the Irishman during their first encounter, letting him live only because Murphy said there was more. Much more. He claimed to have found more gold and gems than he could count, but he wouldn't tell Carlos where.

If Carlos could get away, he had a start point. It couldn't be all that far from where he met Murphy and now that he knew more about the cross – it came from a famous ship – he had a better idea where to look.

Murphy wanted to convert the uncut gems into cash, something Carlos would have helped him to do while taking the lion's share of the profit. They were to meet the next day when Murphy would bring along more of what he had. Ramirez, a back alley con artist well-used to ripping people off, was planning to rob Murphy – it wasn't as if the man could go to the police.

However, perhaps sensing that he had enlisted the wrong person to help him, Murphy fled, and it was only through chance that Ramirez saw him running across the docks to sneak on board the giant cruise ship as they loaded cargo into its hold.

Ramirez hadn't been swift enough, or sufficiently sneaky, because he couldn't get on board and had to watch as the ship sailed into the distance. Unwilling to be defeated, and motivated by the promise of millions, Ramirez flew to the ship's next destination and bought a ticket.

He spotted Murphy trying to get off, the Irishman's confident smile failing when in turn he saw Ramirez waiting for him.

It took Ramirez three days to find Murphy, eventually catching up to him below deck. Murphy tried to call for help, and then fought, despite his emaciated state. His death had been an accident and not what Ramirez had planned.

Silvestre was confident Murphy had no idea what he had found. However, from the description he gave, his words echoing beyond the grave when retold by Ramirez, it sounded like it was everything the San Jose had in its hold when it supposedly sank.

When in their struggle, Ramirez killed Murphy, he took the cross from the Irishman's body, but could find no trace of the gems. Xavier Silvestre could hear the half-truths in the words of his captive and suspected he knew more than he was letting on. Half an hour later, he was satisfied that there was nothing left to learn. He had been in Morocco, but Ramirez did not know the exact location of the San Jose's lost treasure.

The location surprised him, he always figured it was either in Spain somewhere or possibly in England, since two pieces from the original inventory loaded into the San Jose's hold had turned up there. There was still much work to do, but Silvestre felt a step closer than he had ever been before.

The trail went cold at a cruise ship called the Aurelia so that was where he was heading now.

It was due to dock at one of the Canary Islands shortly, his valet, Gomez, had found it for him and arranged a ticket. There was the small matter of the professor to take care of and the cross would have to vanish along with all records that it had ever been at the museum. However, Silvestre was content that he was firmly on the trail of the San Jose treasure.

Finally, after years of research and dead ends, he was on the right path and the cross proved that he had been right all along – the British hadn't sunk her, they sunk something else while the San Jose's captain stole the treasure and sailed away into the horizon.

He would find where Murphy put the gems, even if he had to tear the Aurelia apart and kill everyone on board.

Whatever it took.

'So who is the mysterious redhead?' asked Barbie.

We had returned to the task of trying to figure out who had threatened me today. The woman who confronted me was not, however, in the system.

'How does someone avoid being logged on the ship's central registry?' Pippen asked the air.

Baker wriggled his lips from side to side in thought. 'Well, sneaking on board is the obvious answer. That is not a regular occurrence though.'

He was right, incidences of stowaways were almost non-existent. The one we found dead yesterday was the first anyone had recorded in over two years.

Either way, the redhead I was looking for wasn't in the system and finding her was just one of the problems I faced. Upon returning to my suite, Jermaine had made G&Ts for everyone, refreshing glasses as necessary because believe me, mine didn't last long.

Once I downed the first one and settled into a chair with both dachshunds on my lap, I brought up the subject of the complaints. My team was shocked. Actually, everyone was, which was something of a relief. I went on to explain how I knew they were fake, but done cleverly enough that no one could easily prove it.

Then I brought up the email Barbie got, and she explained that my emails had most likely been hacked.

'We can just set up a new account for you, Mrs Fisher, and shift all your contacts across. It's an easy thing to do,' Baker had announced, believing he was presenting a solution.

I told him not to. 'Whoever did this went to some trouble. If we change my emails, or change the pattern of what we are doing, we tip our hand.' My friends were good enough to listen to what I had to say. 'Barbie is going to move out and we will limit our interaction for a while.'

'Until we catch whoever is behind this attack,' Barbie had added.

We fell into discussing who it could be and why, trying to analyse tactics and not getting very far. I had no idea who the redhead was or whether she was part of it. As for the passengers who raised complaints about me, they presented us with a start point for a clandestine investigation, but it wasn't a lot to go on.

We sipped gin and talked cases and were just glad to be at the end of a busy day. Tomorrow would bring fresh challenges.

When they were gone, and I had eaten a light dinner, I let Jermaine know I planned to visit Alistair and would probably stay the night in his quarters.

Alistair met me, with Anna and Georgie at my feet, at the door to the elevator that leads to the bridge. I took his hand and we kissed in the elevator as it rose from the upper deck into the sky above.

In his quarters, after we had chatted for a while and had a glass of wine, I excused myself to visit the smallest room. The dogs were asleep on the couch and wouldn't move unless prompted to do so by the promise of food.

Alistair had bought me that amazing necklace and even though I didn't get to keep it, I knew what it represented. He loved me and I loved him. It was a special place to be.

When I checked my makeup in the bathroom mirror a few moments later, the wrinkle was still there. There was nothing I could do to hide it, but this isn't my first rodeo and there are things one can do that mean you don't have to hide one's imperfections. I was going for distraction techniques.

I dabbed a little perfume here and there and yanked the bathroom door open with confidence and purpose. Then I shrieked because Alistair was standing right outside.

He was staring at me, his eyes wide and his mouth hanging open. Good thing too because I only had on the jacket he asked to see me in, and the boots I borrowed from Barbie. Jermaine had dried them out and polished them until they looked good as new.

He swallowed hard and tried to find his voice which was when I noticed what was dangling from his fingers.

'Oh, my God. Did John give it to you?' I gasped.

Alistair tore his gaze from me to stare at the sapphire necklace as if he had forgotten it was in his hand.

'I, um, I bought it from Mr Oswald Junior. He said his daughter didn't have enough class to inherit it.'

I gasped again, then pulled him into a passionate embrace so I wouldn't be able to ask him how much he paid the second time or berate him for doing so. Somewhere on the ship, there was someone with a vendetta against me. That was the only thing we managed to figure out earlier. Due to the ship's nature, in order to hack my emails, a person would almost certainly have to be onboard.

Who they were and why they hated me was something that was going to trouble me until I figured it out. Except for right now, that is. Right now, Alistair was going to make me forget all my worries.

Epilogue: First Dig Two Graves

Deep in the bowels of the ship, on the lowest of the passenger decks, a figure sat in semi-darkness.

'She ran right past me.' The figure laughed. The comment was aimed at the figure's own reflection, shining back from the mirror in a cramped cabin. More palatial surroundings could be easily afforded, but this was not a pleasure cruise. There was a purpose, a very important one. 'She ran right past me and didn't even notice, so lost in her own importance. Well, Patricia Fisher, mark my words, I have only just begun.'

Sleep would be difficult until revenge was had.

Patricia Fisher needed to suffer. She needed to suffer the way she made people suffer.

'I will destroy you,' the reflection growled. 'First your reputation and your friends. Soon your lover. Let's see how you feel when you are all alone.'

The reflection smiled, if that was what you could call it. The lips split to show the teeth behind them, but it was more a cruel sneer than an actual smile.

Seeing Patricia Fisher had been important. It reminded the figure of the purpose – why it had to put itself through the weeks of hardship and spend so much money. In a moment of self-doubt, just seeing the enemy, the figure's … nemesis, was enough to reinforce the conviction that brought about the decision to seek revenge by such extreme measures.

Leering into the mirror, the figure laughed at the face looking back.

'Oh, you will suffer, Patricia Fisher. You will suffer like a character from the bible, and I won't stop until you are begging me to. That's when I reveal myself, only then, when you are ready to understand why. You deserve everything you have coming and more.'

Gripped by rage, the figure lashed out with a fist, smashing the mirror. Shards fell out to litter the tiny dressing table built into the wall and the figure rotated a hand to confirm the sting of pain was indeed a piece of the mirror's glass embedded in a knuckle.

Pulling it free, the figure licked the blood from the shard and let out a little giggle.

'Oh, yes, you will suffer.'

The End

Author's Note

Writing the end of my sixty third novel occurred just after I returned from a big independent author conference in Las Vegas. I have jet lag working in my favour, so it is nearly midnight, and my brain thinks it is early evening.

The conference was a smash because I got to see some of my hardcore fans. Having fans is a crazy concept for me. I get that my books are fun to read – they are supposed to be. I do my best to fill them with madcap situations that will amuse my readers, but gaining readers who would like them enough that they would travel to meet me?

I find it truly humbling.

I got to speak at the conference too, trying my best to inspire fledging and hopeful authors. They want to write more books, so I explained some of the tactics I employ to get more words down than I otherwise might.

Now a little about the book.

The mystery of the stowaway and the cryptic enigma of the person in the epilogue will be revealed in good time. I, for one, believe a series needs something to tie the books together, a solid subplot that makes readers want the next book.

I am not a fan of cliff-hangers though and will employ them only rarely and when I feel it is absolutely necessary. Hopefully, I got the balance right here and you are left with a satisfactory ending even though you keenly want the next part of the story. Subplot – it makes a series into something more than a collection of related books.

I need to get to bed soon, I have work to do in the morning and a bunch of decisions to make. I interviewed two ladies from my village today, both looking to fill the role of administrative assistant. I have more people to interview yet, but might hire more than one because I have that much work to offload.

All I want to do is write, but the nature of the beast is such that I have to market and advertise if I want to sell books. Then there are twelve dozen other things that get in my way such as handling the big bookshops, translations, website, promotion sites … it's another long list. I will be steadily handing these tasks out when I start hiring people so that I might focus more consistently on the words.

We shall see what comes, but I definitely need some help.

I am off to write the next book in this series now - my brain is wired for Patricia, and I hope to get a few in this series under my belt before I move onto Rex and Albert or Felicity and her pets, or even to the Blue Moon crew. I just finished a Realm of False Gods book before this one, so they are getting a break while I focus on cozy mystery.

Take care.

Steve Higgs

PS – Don't forget to check the next page to see the next book in this series and get the FREE offers.

What's Next for Patricia Fisher

What's worse than one dead body? Two, right?

Wrong.

It's not so much the number of bodies that Patricia needs to worry about, it's how far up the mystery meter they score, and this latest case is a doozey.

Confused by the clues, Patricia and team must work against the clock to discover the truth, and now they know what is going on, they must race against the clock to stop the killer getting away with it.

Steve's Bestselling Series

Baking. It can get a guy killed.

When a retired detective superintendent chooses to take a culinary tour of the British Isles, he hopes to find tasty treats and delicious bakes …

… what he finds is a clue to a crime in the ingredients for his pork pie.

His dog, Rex Harrison, an ex-police dog fired for having a bad attitude, cannot understand why the humans are struggling to solve the mystery. He can already smell the answer – it's right before their noses.

He'll pitch in to help his human and the shop owner's teenage daughter as the trio set out to save the shop from closure. Is the rival pork pie shop across the street to blame? Or is there something far more sinister going on?

One thing is for sure, what started out as a bit of fun, is getting deadlier by the hour, and they'd better work out what the dog knows soon or it could be curtains for them all.

More Books by Steve Higgs

Blue Moon Investigations

Paranormal Nonsense

The Phantom of Barker Mill

Amanda Harper Paranormal Detective

The Klowns of Kent

Dead Pirates of Cawsand

In the Doodoo with Voodoo

The Witches of East Malling

Crop Circles, Cows and Crazy Aliens

Whispers in the Rigging

Bloodlust Blonde – a short story

Paws of the Yeti

Under a Blue Moon – A Paranormal Detective Origin Story

Night Work

Lord Hale's Monster

The Herne Bay Howlers

Undead Incorporated

The Ghoul of Christmas Past

The Sandman

Jailhouse Golem

Shadow in the Mine

Ghost Writer

Patricia Fisher Cruise Mysteries

The Missing Sapphire of Zangrabar

The Kidnapped Bride

The Director's Cut

The Couple in Cabin 2124

Doctor Death

Murder on the Dancefloor

Mission for the Maharaja

A Sleuth and her Dachshund in Athens

The Maltese Parrot

No Place Like Home

What Sam Knew

Solstice Goat

Recipe for Murder

A Banshee and a Bookshop

Diamonds, Dinner Jackets, and Death

Frozen Vengeance

Mug Shot

The Godmother

Murder is an Artform

Wonderful Weddings and Deadly Divorces

Dangerous Creatures

Patricia Fisher: Ship's Detective

Fitness Can Kill

Death by Pirates

Albert Smith's Culinary Capers

Pork Pie Pandemonium

Bakewell Tart Bludgeoning

Stilton Slaughter

Bedfordshire Clanger Calamity

Death of a Yorkshire Pudding

Cumberland Sausage Shocker

Arbroath Smokie Slaying

Dundee Cake Dispatch

Lancashire Hotpot Peril

Blackpool Rock Bloodshed

Kent Coast Oyster Obliteration

Felicity Philips Investigates

To Love and to Perish

Tying the Noose

Aisle Kill Him

A Dress to Die for

The Realm of False Gods

Untethered magic

Unleashed Magic

Early Shift

Damaged but Powerful

Demon Bound

Familiar Territory

The Armour of God

Terrible Secrets

Top Dog

Free Books and More

Get sneak peaks, exclusive giveaways, behind the scenes content, and more. Plus, you'll be notified of Fan Pricing events when they occur and get exclusive offers from other authors because all UF writers are automatically friends.

Not only that, but you'll receive an exclusive FREE story staring Otto and Zachary and two free stories from the author's Blue Moon Investigations series.

Yes, please! Sign me up for lots of FREE stuff and bargains!

Want to follow me and keep up with what I am doing?

Facebook